WAKING PARTNERS

WAKING PARTNERS

Gerald Hammond

Severn House Large Print
London & New York

This first large print edition published 2008
in Great Britain and the USA by
SEVERN HOUSE PUBLISHERS LTD.,
9-15 High Street, Sutton, Surrey, SM1 1DF.
First world regular print edition published 2007 by
Severn House Publishers, London and New York.

British Library Cataloguing in Publication Data

Hammond, Gerald, 1926-
  Waking partners. - Large print ed.
  1. Traffic accidents - Fiction 2. Attempted murder -
  Fiction 3. Detective and mystery stories 4. Large type
  books
  I. Title
  823.9'14[F]

  ISBN-13: 978-0-7278-7682-9

Printed and bound in Great Britain by
MPG Books Ltd, Bodmin, Cornwall.

One

In business, Aubrey Merryhill was a very cautious man. His business had started small and stayed the same. In that manner, he limited his profits but also his risks. He had no particular desire to die rich, though the arrival of Lynne into his life had led him to consider whether he should not perhaps raise his sights a little. Instead, he had taken out insurance policies on his life.

Aubrey had been the afterthought of a couple of parents who had been perfectly happy without him. When he had graduated from college with a smattering of Italian and a modest degree in Business Studies, both had already passed on, leaving him a modest legacy that had been only partially swallowed up in fees and subsistence. This might have been his misfortune. Vast sums are hardly ever accumulated by the person who already has something to lose, but the pauper can afford to be more adventurous and to speculate – with somebody else's money.

While Aubrey had been wondering what to do with his life, he had met an Italian businessman who was looking for a British agent. Aubrey had found himself, almost without intent and with very little persuasion, the importer of a range of high-quality Italian leather goods, despite his inexperience in such areas. This hadn't seemed of great concern to the Italian, who had been happy to trust that Aubrey would learn the ropes soon enough. It was not a difficult role, as the client list of retailers was already established and the goods almost sold themselves; so Aubrey had little to do but receive consignments of the goods, accept the orders from retailers, match the one to the other, ship out the goods and collect the money. His office had grown in parallel to the growth of the Italian firm, but the work was not demanding and he was sublimely uninterested in the blandishments of other small foreign firms in need of an honest and businesslike agent.

Only in his driving had he shown a streak of adventure. Speed held no terrors for him.

People could let you down but in a good car he knew that he was in command. He thrilled to the response of a pedigree machine to his demands. His vintage MG had been maintained in mint condition by his own efforts, with occasional help from a specialist firm. He usually drove it with the top down and the windscreen folded flat to minimize wind resistance, and the car responded with an extra surge of acceleration. His horn-rimmed Reactolite glasses served instead of goggles. He had found the car rusting in a farmer's barn and so far its renovation had cost him the price of a Lotus Esprit; but he did not grudge a penny of it. It was responsive to drive and, in his eyes, smart to look at. He was blind to the comparative discomfort of the ride and to the fact that a man in middle age did not maintain his dignity in a teenager's toy.

He could have travelled between his home and his business by way of a main road, but that road was almost straight and carried a lot of traffic. Far more enjoyable was a minor road that might once have been an important part of the rural network but had long been bypassed. It was so hemmed in by trees that for much of the journey he was driving along a living tunnel that opened up wherever the deep gully of Willow Water was nearby.

Aubrey knew every hollow, every change of camber that the road could offer him, and he treated them as his slaves. The bends had been put there for his entertainment. He could hear his tyres sing, accompanied by the music of the exhaust. The trees appeared, grew, swept past and fell back. In his own mind he was Fangio or Hill or one of the Schumacher brothers.

On this occasion he glanced down fondly at his flatcoat retriever, sitting upright in the passenger seat, supremely confident and enjoying the wind despite the whirring of his ears. There was a critical speed at which Xanthic always lowered his head out of the wind and Aubrey was curious to discover it, but the critical speed varied with the air temperature. The road before them rose to an uphill stretch, so he put his foot down, glancing down again at the dog. Thus he failed to recognize disaster as it rushed at him.

Paul Fletcher had been blessed with the middle name of Juniper, which he never used or even admitted to. When he asked his single-parent mother the reason for this unusual appellation, she only blushed. He was tall, thin and no longer given to spots. His head was aquiline, but its appearance was softened by an expression of friendly benevolence and a head of hair that flopped lankly over one eye.

Paul had taken a degree in business studies. He had begun his working life as office manager and general gopher to an entrepreneur whose speciality was the buying up of bankrupt businesses and setting them back on their feet. Unfortunately the entrepreneur had bought up one business that was bankrupt because it was seriously non-viable and, worse, had poured money into his attempts to salvage it. He had followed the business into Queer Street. Paul had found himself on the labour market, but he had been well taught by his first employer and by experience.

Aubrey had needed a chief clerk and general assistant. The job centre had sent Paul to him. They had got on well. Aubrey had liked Paul's eager, adventurous mind. He had given him the job and then proceeded to stifle that mind. Paul had fretted.

He could see ways in which Aubrey's business could be streamlined, expanded and generally given a shot in the arm, but the result of any such suggestions was usually an approving smile, a pat on the arm and the words: *We don't do it that way,* or *That would never work.*

Almost every day, Paul considered leaving; but the money, if not good, was adequate; he liked Aubrey and he had a very satisfactory relationship with Julie Watts, the firm's receptionist, secretary, telephonist and typist. Paul's mother had left him a small house in the outer suburbs of London, which had sold well, so that Paul had been able to buy a rather better house near his work and to the east of it. It was part of his experience that anyone living west of his workplace was always driving into the sun.

Julie was the daughter of a couple of university lecturers. She was a genuine strawberry blonde with pert features and a figure that turned heads. She had learned early in her life that sex was fun. She enjoyed flirtation, relished the first kiss, welcomed the caresses that followed and gave herself up totally to the internal massage that consummated the

10

event. For these reasons she had been expelled from two successive prestigious schools. With that record behind her and a singular lack of successful examination results, there had been a general disinclination of establishments of further education to open their doors to her. A secretarial college, however, had failed to ask the right questions and taken her on trust. Her natural dexterity with a keyboard had helped her on her way and a curious and enquiring mind had done the rest. She had soon achieved a platonic relationship with the word processor. Typing and filing required little mental effort and so fell well within her capabilities.

Her father had begged her almost tearfully to mend her ways for the honour of the family and then approached Aubrey Merryhill in search of a job for her. Her mother, on the other hand, had sat her down in a hard chair and, leaning over her so that she could not get up again, had read her a lecture that included such matters as the most certain ways to avoid pregnancy or disease and a long description of what would happen to her if she failed to follow, as a nice girl should, her mother's advice.

Julie had a good telephone manner and a charming smile, thus completing the qualifications required of a secretarial telephonist-cum-receptionist. She had hit it off immediately with Paul Fletcher. Her father, in desperation, had agreed to make her an allowance equal to her salary as long as she remained in approved employment. It was tacitly understood that employment with Aubrey Merryhill would be approved but that many other jobs might not.

She and Paul had soon moved in together. Her father, only too pleased to have her out of sight and almost out of mind, was comforted by his wife's assurance that Julie knew not only about the birds and bees but also about such equally important life forms as babies and viruses and he had turned a very blind eye.

Paul would never have claimed to be in love, but Julie was attractive in daylight and skilled in the dark. He was a young man, full of vigour and with no other attachments. She suited him very well.

Life, on the whole, was good.

Aubrey's business was located in a former mill. The Mill – still the name it was known by – could have looked grim, a reminder of a less easygoing industrial past, but its appearance was now softened by a thick cladding of ivy. The ivy might have been harmful to the stonework, but the local birdlife appreciated it.

As Lynne Merryhill approached the building, Julie and Paul were closeted together in the latter's small office. Julie was standing beside his chair – not as a mark of respect but so that he could more conveniently slide his hand up and down the inner side of her leg. It had become her habit to take dictation standing up. Paul was a young man at the height of his sexual vigour and he was easily tempted.

Lynne Merryhill had entered her forties but without losing her figure or much of her looks. She had more than her fair share of intelligence, though she hid it well on the grounds that nobody likes a bluestocking. Her accent was pleasingly middle-of-the-road, not provoking anybody by being either too la-di-da or too workaday. Her words, on the other hand, were usually well chosen but sometimes outspoken with the intention of giving a shock to anyone whom she suspected of not giving her proper attention.

If Mrs Merryhill had delayed her arrival by a few more minutes or walked more quietly, she might have intruded on a scene that would have stretched her tolerance to its limit. As it was, she found an apparently decorous scene. Paul was in the middle of dictation and his hand was back in his pocket and fumbling with a handkerchief.

The figure that Lynne Merryhill had retained was well rounded and of slightly less than average height, topped by a mildly anxious face and a neat cap of dark hair. Paul knew her as a considerate lady with excellent manners whose tongue often got away from her. There were times when her outrageous remarks almost shocked him yet lent her a certain charm by lifting her out of the ruck of the inhibited.

She had trained as a nurse and had begun her nursing career in the local hospital. But her father had died and her mother had decided that she was too frail to manage without the services of her nursing daughter. Lynne had nursed and pandered to her mother for years until freed by the latter's death – from an illness totally unrelated to the symptoms that she had been complaining of for all those years. It had then turned out that her mother had been living on an annuity.

Lynne had gone back to work, but nursing had changed. She had begun a course in accountancy, but had given up before the end and become a bookkeeper. It had seemed that time had passed her by, until she had met Aubrey Merryhill on a Liberal Party picnic.

Paul's room was small, too small to accommodate three people simultaneously. 'Come through into Aubrey's room,' she said. Julie noticed that Lynne's round face was suddenly haggard. Bringing up the rear, Paul was only concerned to make sure that he and Julie were presenting respectable faces to the world. The two looked at each other in puzzlement.

Leading the way, Lynne was unaware that her companions were walking on trembling knees. After a momentary hesitation she seated herself behind her husband's desk. Paul and Julie took the visitors' chairs.

Lynne looked at each of them but with unseeing eyes. 'When you phoned this morning,' Lynne told Paul, 'I had nothing to tell you except that he had left home as usual.

15

When I got the news a few minutes later, I waited until I had something definite to say. And I'm afraid it's not good. On his way here this morning, my husband crashed his car at the bend above Willow Water. He is badly injured.' She fell silent, toying with a paperweight on the desk.

'How... How badly?' Julie asked.

'It's bad. He's alive. He has severe brain damage and they say that his injuries are too severe to permit an operation yet. He's in a deep coma.' Lynne's voice was shaking despite an obvious effort to retain control. 'They've taken him to St Thomas's, where they have the skills for this sort of emergency.'

'Do you have the ward number?' Paul asked.

Lynne managed a faint smile. 'If you're thinking of sending a card or fruit or something, that's very good of you, Paul. But Aubrey wouldn't know. They don't expect him to come out of it for a long time...if he ever does. They don't seem very hopeful, but they're giving him every chance. What they did say is that a patient in a coma hears and even remembers quite a lot of what's going on and that a familiar voice can be a big help. I suppose it gives them something to hang on to and to struggle towards. So I've arranged to go and stay with my sister Mavis in Chelsea. That way, I can spend most of my time with him.

'Paul, you'll have to run the firm, at least for now. We both have faith in you. I already had the authority as Aubrey's partner and I've written you out a letter authorizing you to take charge.' She paused while she removed a long envelope from her handbag and laid it on the desk. Then she hurried on. 'He used to say that the firm ran itself and that it generated quite enough income for our modest needs. I have enough money to be going on with, but I have a feeling that if...when...Aubrey begins to make progress, there may be expenses. I don't know what, but we don't have health insurance; the National Health has its limitations and if you want the best you have to pay for it. I...I'm sure you'll do your best. Phone me in the evening or before nine in the morning if you have problems. My sister's number's in the letter.'

'You'll keep us posted?' Paul said.

'Of course.' Lynne's control was slipping. Her voice choked. 'I'll let you know as soon as there's a change.' She blew her nose, then jumped to her feet and hurried out of the office. They heard a car door close.

'Wow!' Paul said. 'This needs thinking about.'

'I don't know that I'm capable of rational thought,' Julie said. 'You've got me much too steamed up. Let's have a quickie before we get down to it.'

Paul looked at her in surprise. He knew that her carnal appetite was prodigious – Queen Aholibah was said to have had a similar problem – but this was startling. 'Now is hardly the time. Anyway, where would we go? You hate to lie on something hard.'

'I could kneel for you,' Julie said. Her breath was coming quickly.

Paul was unsure which would be the more distracting to contemplate: sex or his new responsibilities. Either might render the other unmanageable. Perhaps a few minutes of total relaxation might allow him to tackle the firm's problems afresh. 'Come on, then. Paper store.'

Two

There was an hour of the working day remaining when Paul Fletcher, feeling calmer than when he had received the first shock of Mrs Merryhill's bombshell, invited the whole staff to join him in Mr Merryhill's room, now temporarily at least his. Mr Merryhill had never believed in spending money on his own comfort, so the room was plain, the furniture serviceable and the carpet dull and badly worn. Even the computer on the desk was dated and had a dispirited look. The chair behind the desk had long since ceased to swivel and had been known to subject its occupant to a sudden descent, but this was all so familiar to the staff that not one of them noticed it any more. It was simply the way things were.

The firm's efforts were directed to no more than receiving orders, taking delivery

19

of consignments, storing, despatching the goods ordered, invoicing, collecting the money and apportioning it between the manufacturer and the firm. The entire staff, therefore, consisted of Paul and Julie, Alma (the bookkeeper), Moira Blessed (who oversaw invoicing and despatches), two young men, Duke and Dave, in the warehouse (who kept track of the stock and produced it, clean and in good repair, when required), and Garry Streen (who lurked behind a screen and was responsible for packaging and labelling of goods). Even so, more chairs had to be brought in from what was grandly known as Reception.

It was not an impressive workforce, Paul decided. Aubrey Merryhill had preferred to have young staff around him. They were cheerful and attractive and less demanding in wages than their seniors. A smattering of Italian was an added advantage and at least the young were capable of learning. Only Alma Jenkinson, the bookkeeper, could be said to have reached full maturity and she was believed to be only somewhere in her late thirties or early forties. It was wrongly believed that she had suffered a disappointment in love and had turned to the Church for comfort. Duke and Dave were distinctly scruffy and, in Duke's case and that of Garry Streen, given to face-piercing.

Paul cleared his throat. This brought him to the attention of the company, which had not been his immediate intent. He was well versed in management theory and thought he knew exactly what he had to say, but the need to say it aloud, to get it right and to stick to it without any mind-changing he found daunting.

They were looking at him, waiting for the words of wisdom. Or for him to fall on his face. He kept his voice low; otherwise it would have become a squeak.

'Mr Merryhill has been in a car accident,' he said.

There was a sudden stillness, as though time had stopped. Few of the staff had known Aubrey Merryhill as more than a mildly benevolent figure who asked after their well-being without listening to the answer and gave orders disguised as requests. In most cases, worry about their own employment prospects outweighed any concern for their employer.

'A bad one?' Dave asked.

'Very bad.' Paul realized that he now had a

clear idea of what he wanted to say. Perhaps the few minutes of relaxation had been a good idea after all – *reculant pour mieux sauter*. 'Now let me tell it in my own way or we'll get muddled. Questions later. As you probably know, Mrs Merryhill was here half an hour ago. The boss has been taken to London and he's in intensive care. We don't know if he'll get better or when that'll be. Meantime, I've been left in charge. Mrs Merryhill promises to let me know as soon as there's any change. She'll be staying with her sister, where she'll be handy for the hospital.

'The boss has always refused to expand or to branch out, but Mrs Merryhill dropped a strong hint that he may need expensive treatment and that what he needs he'll get. So we'd better try to have some ready cash available. You two' – he nodded to Dave and Duke – 'can look through the warehouse for unsold stock. There's usually been something left over after each line was superseded, sometimes a dozen items or more. Give me a list and we'll see what we can sell. And Miss Jenkinson, could you manage a cash-flow forecast – money we're due, less what expenditure we have to make?'

Alma Jenkinson bowed graciously. 'It will be on your desk by tomorrow night. Sooner, if Moira can go to the bank for me and help me with the wage packets.'

'Of course,' Moira said.

'Thank you. Questions?'

It had been too much to absorb quickly and his snipe at Dave had closed their mouths. Duke raised his hand at last. 'How bad is the car?'

Paul had completely forgotten the car. It was unimportant compared to Aubrey Merryhill, who had been a father figure to him even if he could see the flaws in his patron's methodology; but the car was Mr Merryhill's ewe lamb, perhaps substituting for the family he had never had, and might still represent a redeemable asset. 'Good point. I'm going to see the traffic cop who's in charge and I'll find out. I'll also have to see the bank manager and I'll write to Giatelli in the morning. In the meantime, you may care to think about ways in which we can maximize the firm's profit so that we can meet whatever medical costs Mrs Merryhill may incur. He's been a good boss – I hope he still is – and if we pull together...'

He ran out of words, but Miss Jenkinson said, 'Hear hear,' and there was a murmur of agreement.

In Paul, post-coital lassitude was making a belated appearance. But it was not a time for unwinding. He should not have allowed Julie to lead him astray during working hours, he told himself. He recognized that part of his mind was eager for action and wanted to dash about, phoning people. But he was not yet comfortable enough in the saddle to say, 'Get the hell out of here,' and his audience seemed to be waiting for something else.

Moira Blessed raised her hand. She was the youngest of the staff and painfully shy. The attention often drawn to her by her blonde prettiness only increased her shyness. From her first day in the job she had fallen hopelessly for Paul, considering him to be the very summit of masculine perfection. A word from Paul could reduce her to jelly and the idea of addressing him in front of others terrified her, but he had asked for help so help he would get.

'Yes, Moira?'

Moira began speaking, but so softly as to be inaudible.

'Speak up,' Paul said kindly.

Moira cleared her throat and tried to shout, with the result that she became quite audible. 'Some of the bigger stores have been suggesting that they could increase their orders. I mentioned this to Mr Merryhill but he only ever said things like "Always keep them wanting more", and "I don't want to get landed with a lot of expensive, unsold goods". But I know that Blossom's in particular have been buying handbags that aren't as good, and they're definitely paying more for them. Not a lot, but...' She became inaudible again.

'That's the kind of thinking we want,' said Paul. 'Sound out your contacts tomorrow and find out if they're genuinely keen. And ...who has the best Italian?'

The staff looked at each other. 'Probably me,' said Alma Jenkinson. 'I go to Amalfi every summer.'

'We'll have a word in the morning. I'd like to know whether Giatelli could increase our allocation. Anything else?' He looked around. He couldn't have said how he knew, but the room had changed. The atmosphere was charged with hope. More than hope: there was a sense of rising to a challenge, one that had been missing for too long. 'One more thing,' he said. 'This is a word of general advice but I want you to take it seriously. It's this. We'll each have to take more initiative from now on. If there's something you don't know that you ought to know, it's always a temptation to shut up and look wise while you hope that the information will fall into your lap. I've made that mistake myself, more than once. Let it be understood that such evasions hardly ever fool anybody. I'll respect you more if you come out with it and ask for explanations. Anything else? That's all for now, then.'

The others filed out. Paul and Julie were left. She crossed her legs carefully, allowing him a generous glimpse of pink lace under the businesslike skirt.

'I love it,' Paul said, 'but save it until we get home. I want to speak to the police, Traffic Division. See who you can get hold of. I want to talk to whoever looked into Mr Merryhill's accident and I want to know about his car.'

26

Three

The control room spoke to the traffic inspector. He was still at the site of the crash and would see Mr Fletcher there if he went straight away. It was not far off their way home – two sides of a triangle instead of the hypotenuse.

Across the rough and weedy mill yard was another, similar though smaller building, where Ernest Hendry, with a very few helpers, did small metalwork. Much of his trade was casting small souvenir figurines that were then delicately painted at home by outworkers and sold to the tourist trade. He had a special line in soldiers of many different armies, sold ready painted or with painting instructions. Collectors set great store by them.

Ernest came out to meet them. He was a thin man in his forties, red-haired and nervous. 'I heard about Aubrey,' he said. 'Is it bad?'

'As far as I know, yes,' Paul said.

'You've been left in charge?'

'It seems so.'

'And the business will continue?'

Paul looked at him in surprise. 'I expect so. It's a bit early to be thinking along those lines, isn't it?'

Ernest looked confused. 'You're absolutely right. Please forget that I asked.' For a moment Ernest had begun imagining all sorts of annoying new neighbours and conflicts, but realized it was not a worry he could voice out loud. 'Send him my best wishes, please.'

'Of course.'

Paul and Julie settled into the elderly Jaguar. It was Paul's car, but in Julie's view it was 'our' car. It was Julie's turn to drive.

'Do you think I should grow a moustache?' Paul asked suddenly.

Julie made the turn into the main road. 'If you can. Why would you want to?'

'To make myself look older, obviously. I'm young to be taking charge, but that wouldn't matter. I can do a lot of business on the phone. But when I have to meet somebody like a bank manager, I'll have to look responsible.'

'That's true. You have a perfectly responsible face as it is, rather like a lecturer or the better sort of politician, but you do look young.' Julie turned her head to look at him. The car drifted and Paul grabbed for the wheel. 'Sorry. I was just trying to picture you with a moustache. What kind? Military? Walrus? Pencil?'

'None of those.' Paul's heart was still thumping, but Julie took these little incidents in her stride when she was driving. If Paul had made such a mistake she would have read him a lecture and brought up the incident regularly thereafter. 'Just a moustache,' he said.

'You have a good mouth. You wouldn't want to hide it. Something horizontal might suit the shape of your face. Of course, a lot would depend on what colour it came in. Some men have black hair and a ginger moustache and that can look awful. Your stubble looks all right, but it may have streaks. Try growing a simple, nondescript moustache and we can try a little topiary work. But no. Trial and error would take too long. Go into a joke shop or something and buy one or two false moustaches in colours much like your own hair and we can try a

29

few shapes. Then I'll tell you which suits you and whether it tickles. You know, there are some advantages in looking young and innocent and easily fooled,' Julie said. 'The person who thinks he can diddle you is the easiest to diddle.'

'You should know. You're a girl.'

'And what's that supposed to mean?'

Paul frowned in thought as Julie made the turn into the minor road. 'I don't know,' he said at last. 'It was just a feeling.'

'Well, get rid of it.'

At least it bought him a few minutes of silence in which to consider his new responsibilities. Ideas were beginning to take shape in his mind. Meanwhile, Julie tucked the argument away in her mental filing cabinet. It might come in useful some day. They were surrounded by mature trees so that they drove, in the reverse direction to that taken by Aubrey Merryhill, through the tunnel of greenery, making it difficult to appreciate that their road was winding along a hillside with a drop on the left to a tumbling stream, and with a slope rising on the right.

'I heard you phoning Mrs Merryhill,' she said. 'How's the boss?'

'Still in a coma. She's going in to talk and read to him. Apparently a familiar voice can help the recovery along.'

'Does a familiar feel do the same? Perhaps I should pay him a visit. He did enjoy a feel of my bum.'

'And you let him?' Paul asked sharply.

So he was jealous, all of a sudden. Well, well! 'Only the first time,' she said. 'He caught me by surprise. I was bending over some invoices and you don't expect it from a respectable older man, not in this country. After that one episode I made sure I didn't get within reach. Some of the younger girls didn't mind. But I might make the sacrifice again if it would help his recovery along.'

'If there's any groping to be done, I'll do it.'

'Promises, promises. You'll have to make an appointment. My diary's getting rather full.'

'Take it while you can get it,' Paul said. 'Mr Merryhill may not be around any more.'

For a few hundred metres the trees gave way on both sides of the road to grass. Then the valley deepened and trees were all around. The site of the accident was not far past the mouth of a farm track where a single willow towered above the stream. The MG stood clear of the road and facing them, almost on a patch of vacant ground, left over from a road-straightening, that seemed to have fallen into use by parkers, lovers and those with overstressed bladders. Cones and a warning sign were being loaded into a police van and a small group of uniformed officers was grouped between the two vehicles. Julie began to pull in. A weary-looking officer with a silver insignia on his shoulder came to the door. Paul lowered his window.

'Drive on. There's nothing to see here.'

'I'm Mr Fletcher,' Paul said.

The officer blinked at him. 'You look very young.'

'Time will put that right,' Paul said.

'I suppose that's so. All right, pull in, in front of the van.'

Julie drove past the van and turned in. Paul got out and looked back. Even from a distance the MG looked remarkably undamaged. With the windscreen folded flat, it looked ready to set off at speed. 'What happened?' he asked.

The officer looked uncertain. 'You're not a

relative.' It could have been taken for a question.

'No, I'm not. But Mrs Merryhill has left me in charge of the business.'

'I'm afraid—'

'And that,' Paul continued triumphantly, 'includes the car. It belongs to the firm.'

The policeman was not wholly convinced. On the other hand, he was rather short of people to question. 'My car will be back shortly,' he said. 'Meantime, perhaps we could take a seat in the back of yours. The lady is...?'

'My secretary.' Paul decided to stretch the truth a little. 'She's very discreet.'

Paul and the officer got into the back of the Jaguar. The leather was very worn but the seat was comfortable. The officer gave a sigh of relief. He had been on his feet for rather too long. He acknowledged Julie's greeting monosyllabically.

'In brief,' he said, 'Mr Merryhill seems to have met with an accident at about ten past nine this morning. I'm looking into it. Tell me about Mr Merryhill.'

Paul was well aware of the habit of police-men of gathering information while being uninformative themselves. It was a habit that he had no intention of condoning. 'Yes, of course. But first, the car seemed very little damaged. I thought that the accident was serious.'

'It was very serious for Mr Merryhill. The car needs some panel-beating to one wing and the suspension straightened that side.'

'We understood that Mr Merryhill's head suffered serious injury,' Paul said carefully. 'It seems difficult to reconcile his injury with such slight damage to the car.'

There was silence. The men had finished loading the van and were standing around; their conversational tones were the only sound, muffled by the heavy bodywork. At last the officer sighed. 'That is exactly the problem,' he said. 'Mr Merryhill's head struck something or was struck. Yet the car suffered little or no damage. A few more yards and it would have gone over the brink and down the hill into the water, but instead it veered across the road and was stalled by contact with that grassy hump. There is a scratch on the passenger's door—'

'Mr Merryhill did that yesterday, coming out of his own gate,' Paul said. 'He was very upset.'

The officer nodded. 'I'm Inspector Gibbins, by the way,' he said. 'And I may as well tell you that I have asked my CID colleagues for help. I have also requested the Met Police to send a specialist officer to the hospital, to secure any samples from Mr Merryhill's person or clothing and to interview him if he happens to regain consciousness, though that seems unlikely. And I want him examined for the effects of drugs.'

'What do you suspect?'

'I can't honestly say that I suspect anything in particular. I'm not happy with this as an accident. It's just possible that some vehicle passing in the opposite direction threw up a stone – but only just; and if that's what happened, we haven't found the stone yet. The wound to his forehead was straight across and looked clean.'

'If you're visualizing somebody standing in the road with some sort of club,' Paul said, 'you can leave us out of it. We arrived at work together just after eight thirty and spoke with each of the staff over the next half-hour.'

'Was that normal?'

'Absolutely routine. I like to be sure that they're in, awake, sane and sober.'

'Does Mr Merryhill have any enemies?'

'None that I'm aware of. Julie?'

'I'm sure that he doesn't,' Julie said. 'He's a lovely man, always considerate. He always remembers to ask how you are if you've been off sick and if somebody has to take time off for a sick relative he always asks after them. It makes life difficult for some of the younger staff who think they can take time off by inventing a dying grandmother. He never gave anybody anything other than a fair deal. If somebody owed the firm money, he gave them time to pay. In fact, I sometimes thought he was too soft for his own good.'

'He's a bum-pincher,' Paul said.

'But in a nice sort of way,' said Julie. She had been unnaturally quiet during the first part of this discussion and was relieved to be allowed to take part. 'It was never intended as the start to a wrestling match, as it might have been with some of the younger men. Anyway, he'd spent a lot of time in Italy, where a woman feels insulted if her bottom doesn't get pinched now and again. He may have thought that he was being complimentary.'

The inspector did not show signs of being

pleased by this evidence of Mr Merryhill's virtues. He was not getting the answers that he wanted. He could think of many ways in which the accident could have been caused but nothing to explain the head wound. 'Who would you suggest might be better off if Mr Merryhill were to die?'

Paul said, 'You'll have to look at his will to find out who would gain financially. But as to who might be happier, the answer is: nobody that I can think of. His wife seems to dote on him.'

'They haven't been married so very long,' Julie said. 'About five years, I think. They try to look like an old married couple but...'

'But what?'

'I don't know.' Julie frowned. 'There's something deeper. I can tell you one thing: usually the wife of a man with wandering hands will either kick up hell or she'll position herself between those hands and the nearest girl; but she never bothers. It seems out of character.'

The inspector received the information without comment. 'Anything else?'

Paul suddenly remembered something. 'He would have had his dog beside him,' he said. 'He usually did so. Thumping great

37

black flatcoat retriever named Xanthic. I suppose the poor beast took fright at whatever happened and ran off. He was a neutered male but not microchipped, so if you come across him you may have difficulty identifying him. But flatcoats are relatively uncommon. I'll keep in touch with the dogs' home.'

'Would the dog have been wearing a collar?'

'Definitely no,' Julie said. 'The dog got hung up by his collar on a fence once and nearly throttled himself before Mr Merryhill came to the rescue. After that Mr Merryhill said that he'd rather have the dog lost than killed and he would never have a collar on him at all.'

'Thank you,' said the inspector, opening the car door. 'I'll have to make a report. Then, depending on what my superiors make of it, you may have me or somebody from CID visiting you tomorrow for more details and a formal statement.'

'I'll be sure to bake a cake,' Julie said.

'I'm very partial to a Battenberg,' said Inspector Gibbins as he closed the door.

'Drive on,' Paul said loftily, still from the back seat. 'You know, I thought all policemen had their senses of humour surgically removed.'

'Perhaps he grew another one,' Julie said, starting the car. 'He must have known that a Battenberg's one cake that you can't home-bake.'

The next few miles were given over to an explanation of the reasons why a Battenberg cake is impractical for home baking, while Paul thought about the firm's wage structure.

Four

Inside his head there was blackness and, at one step removed, a sort of pain. But he could hear or imagine a voice. It seemed to be a voice that he knew. It came and went. Sometimes it was hollow, sometimes it echoed, but occasionally it was sharp and clear. It was speaking words, but only now and again did the words have any meaning and he could never remember from one to the next.

The High Dependency Unit was quiet except for the barely audible machines and the murmur of Lynne Merryhill's voice in one of the cubicles. For lack of much else to talk about, she had gone back to do-you-remembers and beyond, leaping back and forth in time in a manner only matched in science fiction.

'I've had a long chat with your doctor, the unshaven one,' she said. 'You've had some emergency surgery already, enough to lift the bone fragments. You'll need more, but that must wait until you're strong enough to take it. Meanwhile, he says that the sound of a familiar voice gives the patient something to cling to – something more tangible than life.

'Do you want to cling on? Were you happy? Happy enough to want to claw your way back? Perhaps you used to be. Happiness tends to fade as you get older. All emotion does that. As a child, were you always down in the dumps or high on a mountain top? Childhood's an emotional time, but I don't see you as a very emotional person. Perhaps it's something that we grow out of.

'I was usually a happy child. You can't measure happiness – you can't even define it satisfactorily – but whatever it is I had it.' She sighed. 'I remember the house we had until I was twelve. I could draw you a plan of the house and of the garden, putting in every plant. There was a lawn. It seemed as big as an eighteen-hole golf course to me then, though I suppose it would look much smaller now. A man used to come up from the village to use Dad's motor mower and it took him most of a day to cut the grass, driving round and round in curves and circles, sitting on what looked like a motorbike saddle. I longed to be allowed to drive that mower but I never was. I think that they imagined me driving straight across the flower beds, but I would never have done that. I think perhaps I'll get somebody in to extend our lawn round behind where all those rhododendrons are. Then I could get a motor mower and sit on it. That's the only kind of gardening that attracts me. I love the smell of cut grass.

'We used to have tea on the lawn, from a folding table under a big sycamore, whenever the weather was fine in summer. And it usually seemed to be fine, not like now. We seem to get one or two fine days and then a week of drizzle. Then when it's hot it's too hot. Well, at least you don't have to worry about the weather for a while, in here. It's a nice, controlled, air-conditioned environment for you.

'But they say that the weather only seems to be different because you tend to remember the fine weather and forget the days like today. Today's a day for forgetting – really, you're better off in here. It was raining when I came in. That will make the grass grow. We don't have enough grass to make it worth getting a sit-on mower. I'll have to get Mr Symes in, from the farm. Or perhaps he'd lend me some sheep or geese to keep the grass short. That's what Dad used to do, until he got the motor mower. He had an electric fence that he could put round one section of the lawn at a time to keep the sheep in. I don't know why it worked – I felt the wire, sometimes, and the current hardly even tickled. He didn't bother to charge the battery very often, but once the sheep had learned not to go near the wire, he didn't have to.

'A garden is a splendid thing to have, to sit in or to walk round with visitors, don't you think? But it demands looking after, and always just when other things are screaming for attention. When Dad lost his job because the factory burned down and we moved into a flat, I was sickened at first because I didn't have all that garden to run around and play imaginary games in. But I was still happy. Nobody could make me go and weed a flower bed, because we didn't have a garden, and yet the park was almost opposite and we could play tennis on the public courts. It wasn't like having a court of our own, but it was much better kept. And the public baths weren't far away, so I could always swim.

'They had courts and a swimming pool at the university. I suppose tennis and swimming and squash are exercise that you can take in twos and threes, not like team games and having to get dozens of people out at the same time, which must be problematic when lectures and seminars and tutorials are scattered all round the clock.

'Dad had another job by then, of course, or he could never have afforded the university for me. He was talking about getting another house in the country, with a garden, but he never did. We just stayed on in the flat, which was all right with me. Most of my friends were nearby and some of them had gardens we could laze around in.

'I'd always been seen as bright at school. Learning things was easy, it was just a matter of memory. As you know, I went in for nursing at first. It was satisfying but physically exhausting. My parents were still nagging me to get a degree and like a fool I gave in.

'University was different. They were trying to teach us to think, and it only came slowly

44

to me. I only managed a poor degree in Social Studies. I thought I could walk into a job, but life isn't like that. Those children you have working for you don't know how lucky they are. I know you usually pick the ones with a bit of an education behind them, because they're the ones who are capable of learning and thinking for themselves, but then you only give them donkey work to do, so they get fed up and move on. I know you pat yourself on the back and feel that you've given them a start, a step on the ladder, something to put in a CV, and at least they've had a sight of the world of work. But you have other reasons. You like to have those attractive bodies around. I don't much mind that. You may pinch a few bums – did you think I didn't know? – but you won't get anything more, not with little girls a third of your age. But one of these days you'll find that you've gone too far and one of them will run screaming to Daddy. Or you might have done. Is that what happened? Is this somebody's way of telling you to keep your hands off his darling little innocent?

'After Dad died, my mother decided that she needed me to nurse her. Well, that

45

earned me my keep for a few years. But then she went the way of all parents and I had to look for a job, capitalizing on my degree.

'The only job I was offered was as a junior assistant probation officer. Can you imagine how ghastly that was? Mixing with habitual criminals, always under pressure to let them out into society knowing that they'd only offend again. And reoffending isn't just harm to themselves. Somebody else gets hurt and then who does society blame?

'When you asked me to marry you, I jumped at it. Of course I did. By then I'd worked my way up the ladder, but that only meant more responsibility and more people to rage at me when I got it wrong. I've been ticked off by more judges than a serial rapist has. Anything would have been better than that dismal job. After we married, life seemed dull and I loved its dullness. I revelled in boredom. Nobody was demanding that reports be prepared yesterday. I stopped being the rope in a tug of war between society and the criminal.

'Do you remember our first flat? It was so small that I could get round all the work in an hour. Then I could read the paper or a magazine, watch television or go for a walk in the park. I'd have a meal waiting for you when you came home and I think we were happy.' She lowered her voice further, until the nurse in the next cubicle could hardly make it out. 'I even rather enjoyed the sex. Many wives don't. They talk about it. But I blame the husbands. You took your time and always made sure that I'd come. I appreciated that. Even after that other incident, I could close my eyes and think about Tom Jones.

'That was until you started feeling up the girls you employed. Why did you have to do that? Wasn't I enough for you? Was it just food for your fantasies? Well, I rather think that those days are over. Perhaps my guardian angel thought that he was doing me a favour. On the whole, I wish I could have you back...have *us* back the way we once were. Even if you did pat a few bottoms, what of it? I could still keep you too satisfied to go any further.'

Five

The building was far from beautiful. It had begun as a mill, grinding corn for the villagers and the nearby town. When that trade had been overtaken by bigger and cheaper machinery and more modern firms, it had passed through several transmogrifications, serving time as a linen mill, as a temporary home for bombed-out local government and then as a shoe factory. Now Merryhill Leather Wholesalers occupied the ground and first floors and the smaller basement, and the top floor had just been vacated by a failed workshop that had turned leather into equestrian goods of great quality and no profitability. The second floor had been vacant for several years.

Each of these functions had left its stamp on the building. Industrial archaeologists sometimes visited it out of curiosity, though otherwise it was not well regarded. The waterwheel was long gone and even the millstream had been diverted to feed a trout fishery half a mile away. But the structure was sound; the roof only needed a little attention where grass was sprouting between the blue-black slates. The many uses to which it had been put had resulted in a building full of strange nooks and corners, staircases that went nowhere in particular and protruding nails and hooks that had once served some now-forgotten purpose. The floors were a patchwork with former trapdoor openings filled in by boarding that made no attempt to match the original sturdy oak.

To Paul Fletcher it was suddenly beautified as the old Jaguar rattled and burped towards the rough ground that they flatteringly referred to as the car park, between the Mill and the former store now occupied by Ernest Hendry. It was, if only for the interim, his bailiwick, his stamping ground, his kingdom. It seemed only right that the sun had broken through and bathed the ivy on the otherwise uncompromising structure in a flatteringly golden light. A thrush and a blackbird were busily building nests at opposite ends of the building.

The village through which they had just passed was so picturesque that it verged on the chocolate-box. The houses, grouped around a village green with oak trees, were small, though the occupants resented any reference to them as cottages. The first three or four of them, long since demolished, had been built as adjuncts to the mill. The whole village had been directed towards housing the staff of the mill or the pub and the few shops that had followed. Now, with the mill building employing a much smaller workforce, unemployment had taken its toll and dilapidation was visible except where commuters from the town in search of village life had used the village as a stepping stone on to the housing ladder.

As they entered by the wicket in one of the big doors, it was clear that a fresh mood of willingness, almost eagerness, permeated the place. It was still ten minutes before the nominal starting time. His elders had sometimes engaged Paul with stories of World War Two. They had made much mention of the Dunkirk Spirit. Now, suddenly, he understood what it had meant. Usually, the tiny workforce would be trickling in over the next half-hour, for Mr Merryhill, a late arriver himself, had never been a stickler for timekeeping as long as the work was done and done well; but on this occasion not only were they all in but each seemed to be trying to catch Paul's eye. Somebody was whistling.

He hurried into Mr Merryhill's office. 'Let it be known,' he told Julie, 'that we'll have a discussion, all staff together, in here in an hour's time. We'll try to clear away all the urgents first.'

'Yes, sir, boss.' Julie saluted and goose-stepped outside. Paul watched her go with narrowed eyes. The girl was getting above herself. Perhaps it was time for another spanking. She usually seemed to enjoy it.

He settled to sorting out the papers that he had prepared on his laptop at home the previous evening, to Julie's disgust. (Business for once had seemed more pressing, and even more interesting, than mere dalliance.) He had intended to follow up with several phone calls, but he had no time for more than a quick enquiry to Mrs Merryhill. News of Aubrey Merryhill's injury had circulated in the business community. Julie tried to screen the calls but several of the callers were anxious about money or goods due to them and refused to be fobbed off. Paul found himself explaining at some length that business was about to return to normal. He refrained from adding *if you'll only get the hell off my phone.*

The fourth such call was from the bank manager. They made an appointment. Paul looked up from his diary to see that the staff had filed in and was listening raptly. Even the room – barren, dusty and utilitarian – seemed to have brightened, catching the mood.

He wished them a good morning and then gathered himself. Conducting meetings, and on such new ground, was still strange to him. It had all seemed very clear and logical to him as he had worked it out last night, but would they go along with him? 'I have just spoken to Mrs Merryhill,' he said with what he considered to be suitable gravity. 'There has been no change. I understand that the doctors are pessimistic, but Mrs Merryhill refuses to give up hope.

'Meantime, the business remains in our hands. We have a free hand and a remit to increase profitability as much as we can. Whatever we plan, business must continue for the immediate future along the same lines. If you agree, I propose to dispense, as soon as possible, with fixed salaries. The firm's income will be allocated in proportions still to be determined but based on the proportions over the past two years. One portion would be allocated to running costs and profit, the remainder being divided between us in roughly the proportions of our present wages and salaries. This is so that, if we manage to build up the business, our personal incomes will grow in proportion. And vice versa. In other words, everyone's a partner. The details have to be worked out.'

'Sounds fair,' said Dave before anyone had time to raise objections.

Alma Jenkinson was looking unhappy. 'But who is to guard the interests of the staff?' she asked.

'I had you in mind for that task,' Paul said. 'I think you've just talked yourself into it.' There was a murmur of agreement. Alma shrugged and muttered a few words, but she seemed pleased.

'When would this arrangement begin?' Julie asked.

'As soon as income would seem to allow an increase in the earnings of staff.'

Nobody had comment to make. The idea

of being a partner in a growing enterprise was new and overpowering.

'That's for the future,' Paul said. 'For the moment, who can add to what was said last night?' Several hands went up. 'You first, Alma.'

Alma Jenkinson opened the folder on her lap. 'I have here a current bank statement, a list of outstanding obligations, a list of money due to us less VAT and a list of regular outgoings such as rental, electricity, council tax and of course wages.' She placed three computer printouts on the desk. 'And this is a summary.'

Paul ran a quick eye over the figures. 'At first glance it looks healthy,' he said. 'Take me through it before lunch and meet the bank manager with me at two. If you pin these up on the notice board, anyone interested can look at them. Constructive comments would be welcomed. Anyone else?'

'I haven't quite finished,' Alma said severely. 'I have spoken to Giatelli's in Italy. Their clock is ahead of ours, so I came in early for the purpose. Signor Giatelli has some spare capacity and could increase our allocation. He says that he has been trying to persuade Mr Merryhill to increase his orders.'

Moira shyly raised her hand. 'Just now, I phoned round some of the buyers for the big stores. Fairmile's in Hersham have been wanting to expand into the luxury market. For the dated stock in the basement I quoted two-thirds of the current price and they were ready to jump at it. Two of the others want to increase their order of handbags.'

'Well done,' Paul said. 'We wouldn't be swamping the market?'

'According to *Vogue*,' Moira said, 'the best always sells.'

Paul nodded. 'Three things always sell,' he said: 'the best, the cheapest and the best value for money. I think we have the first and third, so we're moving in the right direction. I suggest that Julie firms up the offers and we'll look at the details before confirming.'

Garry Streen was looking like thunder, but this was so close to his normal expression that nobody had noticed. 'But...' he said.

Paul nodded to him, eyebrows up. Garry, he thought, was a scruffy object, with spots, a sticking plaster flapping loose and clothes that belonged on a bonfire. He would be best kept behind his screen unless they had to turn the whole basement over to packaging. 'Yes?'

'But this is going to make a whole lot more work in packaging and sending out. I'm going to need a raise.'

There was a very faint sound – not quite a laugh but the breath of amusement that a group can produce.

Paul managed to keep his temper. He had known that somebody would miss the point and he had had a bet with himself that it would be Garry Streen. 'I'm sure you can manage,' he said patiently. 'If the packaging and despatch grow beyond what you can cope with in a reasonable day's work, we'll share it out. And if you'd taken in what I was saying you'd have understood that you should be in line for a very good raise if we all work together.'

Garry hesitated. He wanted to protest, but the others seemed to be against him.

Dave was looking uncertain. He and Duke were similar in appearance, each having dark hair worn long, swarthy skin and a prominent nose. But there the resemblance ended, physically and intellectually. Although the two managed to work together well, there was constant hostility in the form of verbal sniping. Duke had an air of street-smart sophistication that was not backed by any intelligence and he had avoided absorbing any education, apparently under the impression that it would damage his virility. Mr Merryhill had taken him on because he was strong, willing and tough enough to deal with any angry callers. Dave was well read and had left college with a degree in design.

'Before we commit ourselves,' Dave said, 'I have a suggestion to make. I've been thinking about it for some time but Mr Merryhill wouldn't consider it.' He spread some paper patterns on the desk. 'Giatelli's handbags are smart and fashionable, but we could make or get better ones by cutting the leather like this.' He made a few quick twists and out of the paper patterns grew a recognizably smart handbag. 'We could get the same balance between suede and polished leather, but it would look slicker, take less work and the cutting pattern would get more bags out of a given area of leather. Also, most women hate the black interior of Giatelli's bags. Most of the makers finish them in black, but for a woman scrabbling in a black lining to find a black purse or notebook among a hundred other black things it's...it's...'

'A pain in the arse,' Alma said bluntly. 'The boy's right.'

Again there was a general stirring of interest. Any new move had gone from being the concern of those directly responsible to becoming a matter of general interest.

'We must follow that up,' Paul said. 'But it will take time and business has to continue now. Dave must work out how long it would take to get up and running with a new design; Moira must estimate how much we can sell and then Julie can order enough from Giatelli to fill the gap. This, I need hardly say, is very highly confidential. Duke must get out the outdated stock, give it a clean-up and examine it for any damage, in case that's why some of it was laid aside. Alma, can you update the figures before Mr Clumber from the bank arrives?'

'I can add in the sale of the outdated stock. Dave's ideas about a new design depends on who makes it and I wouldn't have any idea...'

'I think I can help,' Dave said, 'what they

call a ballpark figure.'

'Fine,' Paul said. 'When we meet the bank manager and other bigwigs, Alma is Director of Finance, Dave is Design Director, I'm Managing Director, Julie is Company Secretary and Moira is Marketing Director.'

'And what am I?' Duke asked.

Dave opened his mouth but was quelled by a glare from Paul. 'These are only names to impress outsiders,' Paul said. 'They don't mean anything; they don't bring any more money. The way I see it, we may have to bring in skilled management help if we can't cope, or we must promote ourselves into what we do best. We've each got to be prepared to learn, and for changes of title as things grow. Duke, you can be Executive Director, if you like.'

Duke nodded, well pleased. 'Up to now,' he said, 'I only done what Mr Merryhill told me. But after what you said I had a good look around. I dug out the leftover goods I knew about. But then... You remember Mr Merryhill had a door blocked off? About three years ago that was. Well there's a couple more small stores cut off. You have to go up a stair and along and down again. And bugger me if I didn't find a dozen and a half of those soft-leather bags with the drawstring they stopped making donkey's ages ago. Very smart, I thought them. I've got all the leftover goods set out on three trestle tables and I'm working my way through them.'

'Well done, the Executive Director,' said Paul. 'We'll take a look after the meeting. Anything else? Right, let's get moving.'

The staff filed out, eager as never before. Paul rubbed his eyes. It was certainly exhausting, having to think for everybody. Virtue had gone out of him.

Six

'There is always hope,' the doctor said doubtfully. 'The most extraordinary things do happen. I put them down to the amazing recovery potential of the human body – and, of course, the skill of my colleagues. Others give the credit to intervention of the Almighty; and that's how tales of miracles are born. It would be going too far to suggest that, if your husband pulls through, my name might go forward for canonization...' He broke off. He had been rambling; and any trace of humour in such circumstances would be the first thing to infuriate the soon-to-be-bereaved and would almost certainly be cast up against him in the event of complaint or litigation. He resumed more carefully. 'It is very rare to be able to say that there is no hope at all. But I'm afraid that this approaches very close to that extreme, or at least there is hardly a chance in a million. And if he should by any chance survive, it is doubtful whether he would have what you or I would call a life.'

'But there is some chance?' Lynne Merryhill insisted.

The doctor shrugged enormously. Doctors were often forced to pronounce authoritatively on matters that were far from definite. He decided to be frank for once. 'It's a matter of judgement, and a very delicate judgement it is. If I was about to throw a coin on to a shop counter, you might well say that there was no chance at all that it would end up standing on its edge, but that happened to me – once. At what point does a chance so slight as to be negligible become a chance? A philosopher might ask: When a man loses his hair, at what point is he considered bald? I think you should seriously consider permitting us to pull the plug. NHS resources, and your own, can hardly be expected to stand the strain indefinitely.'

'Assume that he manages to survive,' she said. 'What happens next?'

'If he manages to survive, he has to become strong enough to survive some serious brain surgery. In that eventuality...'

'Yes?'

'More and more ifs. If the brain surgeon manages to restore some sort of normality to the grey matter and without causing any more damage to the nerves...'

It seemed to Lynne that the doctor at this point left the English language behind and lapsed into the sort of professional jargon that is designed to allow doctors to discuss a patient without revealing their almost total bafflement. He returned to earth at last. 'That would be the start of an impossibly long and hard road with little chance of arriving at a happy conclusion. And, of course, if the patient were to die now, his organs could be donated, if he so wished, but not after a lengthy period on a life-support machine.' The doctor spoke with feeling. He had a number of patients awaiting the donation of bits and pieces from a defunct donor and he had already put in hand the necessary tissue-matching. A simple go-ahead from Mrs Merryhill would mean recovery for those patients.

But it was not to be, or not yet. 'No,' she said firmly; 'as long as there is the merest vestige of a chance of my husband's recovery, I insist on continued life support. He is a good man.'

'The NHS will not continue its support for ever.'

'If that day arrives, I may have to go private.'

Lynne Merryhill entered the High Dependency Unit sombrely, but she soon brightened. A husband who never answered back nor interrupted made the perfect listener. 'Don't you worry yourself,' she said. 'You'll get the best that's going. They don't know everything, these doctors. I remember when my brother Steven was told by the doctor that he had a nasal polyp, but when they got him on the table it turned out to be a deviated septum, whatever that may happen to be. All you've got to do is concentrate on surviving while you heal and healing while you survive.

'The garden's looking lovely just now. The man from the garden centre gave me the best price for coming in and mowing the grass. I was just thinking how nice it will be when you can come home and sit out under the copper beech. You could take your laptop and begin writing that thriller you were talking about. You must have gained something towards it from being an intended murder victim. Because I really can't believe the freak-accident theory.' There was a catch in her voice. She hurried on. 'Everything seems to be going well at the Mill, except that Paul's trying to grow a moustache – to make him look older, he says – and it's coming in lopsided.

'You'll never guess who was asking after you...'

The husk on the bed was prey to an unverbalized wish that the woman, whoever she was, would go away and let him get back to sleep.

Seven

When the big banks recruit staff, they are not looking only for whizz-kids. They have room for only so many in upper management. They recognize that only one in four or five will make it into the upper ranks, so a substantial proportion are chosen from those who will provide competent, loyal service but not feel aggrieved if they are passed over for promotion to the senior jobs. They may rise far enough to become managers of small branch banks, but senior headquarters jobs and the managerships of major branches are not for them. Their cards are marked from the day of appointment.

It had taken Don Clumber several years to recognize that that limitation applied to himself. He had always thought of himself as bright, energetic, a go-getter. When he had been recruited and again when he had been appointed to head the branch where Merryhill did his business, he had thought that he was on his way. But his applications for posts in charge of larger branches seemed to be ignored. He never even made it to interview. Eventually somebody whispered in his ear.

A more volatile man, on learning that his promotion prospects were limited, might have seethed or started seeking more open-ended employment elsewhere; but the accuracy of the selection process was born out by his outwardly calm acceptance. Inwardly, he felt occasional discontent. That discontent increased as developments in telephone and electronic banking led to the closure of many branch banks. It was no longer a secure profession but a thankless one. Nowadays you might not be given the gold watch for staying on but for going away.

When Julie ushered him into the room where Paul Fletcher now held sway, he was nearly forty years old, smartly but conservatively dressed and rapidly losing what had once been a thick thatch of mouse-coloured hair. He could well have summoned Paul to wait on him, but he was curious. He also welcomed any opportunity to get out of an office that had become claustrophobic. His responsibilities had become so familiar that they no longer occupied all his time or much of his attention.

Aubrey Merryhill had always kept his room severe as befitting a restrained and conservative founder of a respectable firm of importers. Paul was looking for a painter and decorator prepared to give the room a new look for little or no profit. At a pinch he might start coming in at weekends with a pot of paint and a roller, perhaps calling for volunteers from among any staff wishing to curry favour with the temporary MD. Meanwhile he was striving to brighten the room by Blu-tacking up some colourful posters and prints.

After the usual handshaking and offers of coffee (refused) Paul explained that Julie remained present as Company Secretary and to take notes. 'We are a small firm at present,' he said. 'Mr Merryhill was always very reluctant to expand. At the moment, however, as I told you on the phone, he is in hospital. He remains in a coma and it seems uncertain that he will ever be able to resume command. Meanwhile, Mrs Merryhill has instructed me to assume control, virtually as the managing director. I have always had authority to sign cheques.'

'You look very young for such responsibility.' Mr Clumber spoke absently. Julie was presenting him with a remarkable view of her legs, from habit rather than any intention to influence the issues. He was a man, and men appreciated these little courtesies.

Paul stroked his young moustache. He could feel it, but it seemed that to others it was not yet conspicuous. 'As I always say, time will put that right.'

'Then I don't quite see where the problem lies,' Don Clumber said, smiling. 'You can draw money for trading and to pay the staff. There is a substantial credit in the firm's accounts.'

Paul leaned back in the swivel chair, which had been treated to some overdue oil and now swivelled to perfection. He laced his fingers over his flat stomach – a gesture that he had seen Mr Merryhill make a thousand times although over a more prominent gut. 'I will explain. Mrs Merryhill has been warned that her husband may need expensive treatment and surgery but that the National Health Service may not be prepared to commit such resources to a cause that only a devout optimist such as herself could consider to offer much hope. She is determined that her husband must have every chance. In the short term, I am to realize assets that include an accumulated stock of goods left over when certain lines were superseded.

'But there is also the long-term position. Mrs Merryhill may need increased income for a long period ahead but, as I explained, her husband always kept the firm and its turnover small. It satisfied his needs so there seemed to be no reason to take risks or to accept stress. He preferred security to the chance of becoming a millionaire. You follow me?'

Mr Clumber nodded vigorously. He had always considered Aubrey Merryhill to be a stuffed shirt. But perhaps this youth would stray too far in the opposite direction? He could read the signs that he had seen so often in the past. A request for overdraft facilities was coming. But if he granted the request and the business then failed, what would be his own position? With that thought there arrived a moment of rebellion. This was the thinking that, moments earlier, he had mentally criticized in Aubrey Merryhill.

'The staff have been aware,' Paul resumed, 'that our principal supplier in Italy would like to enlarge his British market and that big stores in Britain can always use luxury goods, especially quality goods from Italy. We have just confirmed that position over the phone. I'll bring in the lady who now acts as Financial Director. Julie...'

Julie left the room.

'In the longer term,' Paul said, 'we shall be looking at the possibility of making some of the goods ourselves. The remainder of this building lies empty and could be available. One of our staff has training and ideas. But this is at much too early a stage to discuss costings in any detail.'

Alma had been waiting nearby. She and Julie returned. They seated themselves and Julie arranged her skirt carefully to reveal again the same enchantment.

Paul let Alma speak. She laid on the table her summaries of commitments and prospects and her forecast of cash flow. In her personal life Alma had an amusing line of chat, but in the office she was tongue-tied. The quiet bookkeeper, now that she was invited to speak out and found her words given serious weight, was becoming more articulate.

'On the basis of this,' Don Clumber said, 'you never need to overdraw at all.'

'This may prove unduly optimistic,' Alma pointed out. 'It doesn't make provision for what expensive demands Mr Merryhill's treatment may make. We have no way of estimating that. We are also considering a progressive change from importing to manufacturing goods of our own design. Again, it's too early to quote figures, but there would be a substantial outlay followed by a greatly increased profit margin and we hope to go on growing without needing more than a comparatively modest increase in staff. We expect to need a bank loan in about six months' time. We may have a better idea of the amount when we know the medical situation. But we would be very unwise to enter into major commitments without being sure that any necessary overdraft facilities would be available.'

'We'll keep you advised,' Paul said.

'Please do.' But Don Clumber had already made up his mind. Mr Merryhill's firm had been transformed by its founder's absence into the sort of adventurous band in which he could have seen himself thriving, even dominating, if he had only had the courage and the foreknowledge. He was impressed by Paul. Alma Jenkinson seemed to be just the sort of sober, feet-on-the-ground influence that such a body would need. As for that secretary, she might have a twinkle in her eye that was not suited to a company secretary but... He stifled a sigh. Life would be a happier journey if more company secretaries had legs like those and were as happy about showing them.

All in all, this seemed to be a vibrant firm, staffed by eager and intelligent youngsters. So, perhaps, had Microsoft appeared in its infancy. If they came up to scratch, he would back them all the way and tell head office later. Much later. If it should happen that he was witnessing the birth of a successful empire, it might eventually have both room and gratitude for an experienced money man.

'Now,' Paul said, 'you must let me show you the space available and the designs that we're working on...'

Alma returned to her cubicle. Her knees were shaking.

Don Clumber duly admired the first sample handbag. 'Would it be possible,' he asked tentatively, 'to make a briefcase in the same style and materials?'

A glance of surprise flicked between Paul and Dave. 'We'll look into it,' Paul promised. 'If it goes ahead, we'll present you with the first one we make.'

Mr Clumber smiled. 'Don't take too long,' he said. 'My old one is becoming decidedly tatty.'

When Mr Clumber had chauffeured himself away in his nearly-new Ford, Paul sought Alma out in her cubicle.

'Well done,' he said.

'He's going to back us?'

'He's almost inviting us to help ourselves.'

'I did all right?'

'As if you'd been a financial director all your life.'

Alma allowed herself a tremulous smile. 'I'm not used to presenting figures to a banker on behalf of a manufacturer,' she said.

'Get used to it,' said Paul. 'If you go on as you've begun, you'll end up speaking to the World Bank on behalf of ICI.'

Alma went pink with pleasure. She would have welcomed the chance to sacrifice a virgin in his honour.

Eight

Paul and Julie were interrupted in the immediate task of trying to get down on paper a minute of their agreement with the bank manager. The interruption was a phone call from Inspector Gibbins.

'I'm on my way to see you,' he said. 'I trust that that's convenient.' Without giving Paul time to say that it wasn't, he pressed on. 'I understood from you that Mr Merryhill had a dog, which would almost certainly have been with him. I take it that the dog hasn't turned up?'

'Not that I've heard,' Paul said. 'Mrs Merryhill would have told me if he had found his way home. I asked the dogs' home, the vet and the RSPCA to let me know if he showed up.'

'Black retriever, not microchipped?'

'True.'

'Male?'

'Very much so, once upon a time. Now neutered.'

'I think that I have him here. A black dog not unlike a large Labrador turned up, lost, unkempt and wandering, two or three miles from the crash site. No collar. He may have been trying to find his way home. If I bring him along, could you identify him?'

'I think so – if he answers to his own name, which is by no means guaranteed. He has a wonderful nose and a good retrieving instinct but he never was the brightest star in the galaxy. When will you be here?'

'About five minutes.'

Out of curiosity, Paul started the stop-watch mechanism of his wristwatch. Five minutes later, all but a very few seconds, a Range Rover in police livery arrived at the door.

'You may as well go and type it up as far as we've got,' he told Julie. 'And you know the form: finish it off in the same style and format.'

Inspector Gibbins and a black flatcoat retriever, large even for that large breed, entered. It was open to debate who brought whom inside – the inspector was being towed almost off his feet. They were followed by another man in plain clothes.

'Xanthic?' Paul said.

There was no doubt that the dog had been there before. At the sound of his name, and in a familiar voice, he hurled himself forward. He found some fresh purchase on the carpet and the inspector was forced to let go as an alternative to being jerked off his feet. The dog reared up and threw himself against Paul as if preparing to tango.

'That seems to settle that question,' said Inspector Gibbins, laughing. 'The poor tyke has been moping, obviously confused and uncertain. What kind of a name is Zantic? You told me what it means but I've forgotten.'

'Xanthic,' Paul said. 'With an "X" and a "th". I suppose it comes from the Greek. It just means yellow, or golden, or something. Mr Merryhill had a rather old-fashioned education. Come in and have seats.'

'Thank you. But he isn't golden. He's black... This,' Inspector Gibbins said proudly as though performing a conjuring trick, 'is Detective Inspector Mills. He will be taking over as far as any suggestion of foul play is concerned.'

They shook hands and sat. Xanthic was

making a determined effort to climb into Paul's lap but was firmly pushed down. 'Mr Merryhill's dog-of-a-lifetime was a golden retriever called Xanthic. Goldies, curly-coats, flatcoats and Labradors are all members of the retriever family. He decided to name this dog after his deceased favourite, thinking that nobody would recognize the discrepancy. But, of course, he is always being asked what Xanthic means and then having to explain. I must have heard the story a hundred times.

'Now, who do I address on the subject of the car?' Paul enquired of a point roughly midway between the two inspectors.

Each officer looked blank. DI Mills produced a small tape recorder, switched it on and placed it in the centre of the desk.

'I have no objection to this interview being recorded,' Paul said, although the question had not been asked. 'Mr Merryhill's car was very little damaged. It is a valuable vintage car, expensively restored. I am guarding Mrs Merryhill's interests, at her request. I want the car back, without further damage. I do not intend to have it lying around a police garage, rusting, being dented by every passer-by and gathering dust. And the seats were re-covered in the workshop here, using very special leather. I don't want them drying out and cracking.'

DI Mills was a large man, barrel-chested, with black hair, a blue chin and a remarkably deep voice. 'We can't release it yet,' he said. 'The forensic lab is examining it in the hope of finding some explanation for Mr Merryhill's injury. When they are satisfied that they have collected all the available evidence, you'll get it back. But you can't drive it until the suspension's been straightened. Do you want it delivered here?'

'Please. We have secure storage here. While Mr Merryhill's house is standing empty there's always the risk of vandalism. He only has a double carport.'

The policemen nodded understandingly.

Paul could imagine the MG being largely dismantled in the search for truth. The fevered imagination of the forensic scientists and their technicians might imagine hypodermic syringes concealed within the seats or containers of soporific gas hidden almost anywhere. He wanted to utter warnings and threats, but when he came to think about it he recalled that the authorities were well within their rights in searching and that there was no obligation on them to restore such damage as they might have done. Whatever he said might only put ideas into their heads or resentment into their minds. He held his peace except to ask how else he could help them.

The interview opened by going over what had been covered in their discussion at the crash site. Paul, while repeatedly ducking aside to avoid a large, wet, pink tongue, summed it up for them. 'In short, I don't know of anyone with a grudge against Mr Merryhill or with anything to gain from his accident. But then, I only knew him in the office; we didn't socialize at all. Not for any particular reason – we just had nothing in common in particular, and I had a feeling, which I think he echoed, that too much familiarity between a boss and his staff may be a bad thing. Of course, it can also be a good one,' he added, remembering his own affair with Julie. 'It's always possible for two personalities to grate against each other without the friction being obvious to out-siders. I have the impression that Mr and Mrs Merryhill lived quietly without much of a social life.

'You're welcome to speak with any of the

staff, but I think you'll find that we were all here at around the time of the incident and can vouch for each other. Miss Watts and I arrived together. There are only five other staff and I saw and spoke with each of them within a few minutes. Not', he added thoughtfully, 'that that sort of information is likely to be what you're after.'

'Why would you think that?' DI Mills asked sharply.

Paul made an effort not to sigh or to cast up his eyes. 'I haven't been giving much thought to the nuts and bolts of how somebody would set up the accident to Mr Merryhill – if it was set up. I can more easily imagine a large stone thrown up from between the double back wheels of a lorry. But perhaps that's what your men were searching for when I met you at the site?' he asked Inspector Gibbins.

'Perhaps.' The inspector was looking as though Paul had enquired after his infection.

Paul was tempted to meet such stubborn reticence with a similar reserve, but the temptation to show himself capable of expounding on the possible explanations was irresistible. 'If the accident was arranged,' he resumed, 'I really can't see anybody standing in the middle of the road with a pickaxe handle, baseball bat or Indian club. It would be too easy for Mr Merryhill to swerve one way or the other and either avoid him or run him down. Any heavy object thrown at him would give him time to duck. And most other methods would require a fairly accurate estimate of either where or when Mr Merryhill's head would pass a particular point. But I can imagine him being given a powerful dose of a soporific to act as a "knockout drop". On that piece of road he'd be almost bound to go over the brink instead of fetching up where he did, quite gently. The snag to the knockout drop hypothesis is that, as far as I know, he wasn't on any medication, none of us are regular visitors to his house and Mrs Merryhill isn't the sort of person to have access to knockout drops, or anything like that – or the knowledge of how to make them. But I suppose that the post-mortem would reveal if he'd been given any such drug?'

'Eventually, perhaps,' DI Mills said reluctantly. Like his colleague, he was evidently of the school of policemen who felt that, where information was concerned, it was better to receive than to give; but after a moment of thought he decided to stretch a point. 'It can take time,' he said. 'If they know what they're looking for they can home in on it immediately, but an unspecified sleeping drug could require weeks of searching, testing or trial and error.'

'I wish you luck,' Paul said. 'But perhaps you may turn up a witness. Because, if he was given a drug, the culprit wouldn't know where the car would eventually come to a halt. So he or she – the culprit – would have to follow the MG with some kind of blunt instrument handy. In which case I'd suppose that he'd be bound to get traces of blood or skin somewhere about his person or property.'

In the opinion of DI Mills, what Paul did or did not suppose had little bearing on the case. 'Did he always drive around with the top and the windscreen both down and no crash helmet?' he asked.

'In fine weather, yes. In a drizzle, he'd put up the windscreen. It had to be very wet before he'd erect the soft top. He has a hard top in the garage that he can put on when the weather's really foul. He usually has it on during December and January. He always says that the blast of fresh air keeps him healthy. That may be true. I've never known him catch a cold. I don't suppose any germ accustomed to central heating could survive in that atmosphere.'

'You told Inspector Gibbins that Mr Merryhill had no enemies.'

'I'm not sure that I worded it quite so positively. To the best of my knowledge I do still hold that view. But I've been told that he was sometimes free with his hands around the female staff. I suppose enemies could be made that way. You could ask Miss Watts.'

Xanthic had made several more overtures of undying love and been repulsed, so he had settled down under the desk with his chin on Paul's foot and begun to snore. They had managed to ignore the snores, but when the dog stirred and produced a resounding fart the two policemen decided that it was time for them to go and interview the staff.

'That's disgusting,' Julie said on her return, sniffing the now tainted air. 'Does he often do that?'

'Not very. He was probably eating something awful while living rough. I think he sensed that the visitors were holding me up and that I wanted to get rid of them.'

'That would be a guaranteed method,' Julie said. 'But I hope he can do it on demand and at no other time. How did you get on?'

'They wanted to know about his habits. I had to tell them what you'd told me about wandering hands. They'll probably ask you about it.'

Paul opened both windows, so that when DI Mills made a tentative return some time later the odour of flatulent dog was barely noticeable. The DI sniffed and completed his entrance. 'On another subject,' he said, 'may I bring somebody to see you on a matter of business?'

'I suppose so,' Paul said.

Mills refused to be deterred. 'This afternoon, perhaps?'

'I'm rather busy, but I'll fit you in. Make it late afternoon. What's it about?'

'I'll let him tell you himself.'

When they were leaving for home, rather later than usual, Paul's mind was taken up with the proposition that the inspector's brother-in-law had put to him. He had his hand on the car's door handle before he realized that Julie was talking to him. 'What?' he said.

'Yes, I thought you weren't listening. I asked if we were taking that big brute home with us?'

Paul glanced down at Xanthic. 'There's nowhere else he can go.'

'Put him into the kennels.'

Paul spread an old rug on the back seat of the Jaguar and Xanthic obligingly jumped in and settled down. 'You know they said they wouldn't have him again. He howled non-stop last time and chewed the door of his kennel until they had to replace it. We'll have to call in and collect his bed and things. Mrs Merryhill will be staying at home tonight. He has his own teddy bear and she says that he'd be lost without it. Hop in.'

Julie got into the car but she was looking like thunder. She decided that it was high time she put her foot down and asserted herself. 'I don't want him in the house.'

'We don't have an alternative. Besides, I spoke to Mrs Merryhill and she asked me particularly to look after him. She can't possibly take him with her. Her sister keeps cats.'

'I don't see that she has any right to ask such a thing.'

'But I'm happy to do it,' Paul explained, driving off. 'He needn't bother you. I'll do any walking and feeding and brushing. He can sleep in the back lobby.'

'Dogs make me nervous. I was bitten once.'

'Xanthic won't bite you. He might give you a nasty lick. He's the softest lump you could come across. He could probably fetch you to me in those big jaws without making a mark. We'll try it tomorrow.'

Julie realized that when Paul resorted to irony his mind was made up. There was no point fighting a fait accompli but she could take a petty revenge. There would be no sex for Paul that night.

Unhappily for Julie's resolve, Paul's mind was full of other things. He worked late and walked Xanthic. By the time he arrived at their bed, Julie was sound asleep.

Nine

Agnes Mitchell, the nurse on day shift covering Aubrey Merryhill and his immediate neighbour in the High Dependency Unit, was unwed – not, she was wont to say, from lack of being asked. It happened, however, that her sister had married the brother of one of the officers on Detective Inspector Mills's team. That interesting fact emerged in casual chat between officers, but the inspector pricked up his ears. DI Mills's team was carrying a heavy load and was short of staff at the time. Uniformed branch was even shorter-handed.

On consideration, it seemed to Mills that an officer posted to guard a man who, according to the doctors, was likely to die anyway, or else to end up as a human vegetable, would hardly be justified in the face of all the team's other commitments. Nor was there the least likelihood of Mr Merryhill making a statement. On the other hand, the inspector had been told of Lynne Merryhill's dutiful visits and lengthy chats to her husband. He would very much have liked to be a fly on the wall while she was talking to her husband and it was unlikely that Mrs Merryhill would speak a tenth as freely in the presence of a police officer. He therefore approached Agnes through her brother-in-law and met her by appointment in the most respectable hotel thereabouts.

In view of the saving he hoped to make in officers' time, some expenditure on cocktails seemed justified. Soothed by the surroundings and lubricated with alcohol, they were soon on first-name terms – Agnes and Jerry. Detective Inspector Mills's first name was in fact David, but when he had been a detective sergeant it was noticed that the 'DS' in DS Mills might well have stood for 'Dark Satanic', as in Blake's 'Jerusalem'. Immediately, he had become known as 'Jerusalem', or 'Jerry' for short, and the nickname had stuck. He rather preferred it, using it as a conversation-opener on social occasions when all else failed.

He had little difficulty in persuading Agnes to tape-record whatever Mrs Merryhill told her husband's subconscious. Information obtained in this manner would never be admissible in court, but it might tell him where to look. Any cassettes made while Mrs Merryhill was only reading to her husband from what she believed had been his favourite books could be rerecorded. Agnes was also to phone him immediately if any characters that she might regard as suspicious showed any interest in the patient. Agnes, whose life contained little that could be regarded as exciting or even mildly romantic, was happy to accept the commission.

Much of the material recorded was irrelevant and boring.

'Good morning, my dear,' Lynne Merryhill said, kissing her husband on his unresponsive cheek and settling herself into the hard but not too uncomfortable chair. 'They tell me that you're gaining strength and that you may soon be strong enough to take surgery. That's the good news. Whether I should bring you the bad news I don't know. The bringer of bad tidings was sometimes executed, but you're in no position to do that, so perhaps I'll risk it. The doctor couldn't tell me whether somebody in a coma had any chance of understanding what was said to them rather than merely having the sound of a familiar voice to cling to, so I don't think that I need to censor what I tell you with too much care. It's going to be difficult enough to fill whole days at a time with chat without having to filter what I'm saying. So much easier just to treat it as an occasion for thinking aloud.

'The bad news is that most of the damage is underneath or knitted together with blood vessels and nerves that you need in order to stay alive and function. It's very high-risk surgery. They're trying to find somebody within the National Health Service prepared to take it on, at whatever risk to his career...and to you, of course. For the moment, it looks as though the surgery will have to be undertaken privately, possibly bringing somebody from abroad.

'And that, you must see, is going to cost. Whether it would be worth it I don't know. It would be a shame to spend a fortune and not have you back in full mental working order. I don't think that surgeons ever operate on a no-cure, no-fee basis, so it would be like the time that we sent the telly for repair and it cost as much as buying a new one, and when we got it back it couldn't get Channel Four. Current practice is to scrap a TV or a video as soon as it falters and buy a new one, but one can't do that with husbands.

'So there's the question of whether the cost would be justified by the risk element. But there's another factor. You've never been the most considerate of husbands. Perhaps you think, or thought, that you were, but it's been a long time since you gave any spontaneous thought to what I might want, rather than what you might want me to have because it pleased you or made you look good. That's the other part of a rather complex equation.'

She paused. Any watcher, if such there had been, would have known that her mind was miles away. She was still thinking aloud.

'On the plus side is that I might be presented with a blank canvas. By that I mean that, if your memory has been wiped clear of your less desirable habits, I may be able to bring you up again as if you were the child you never gave me. I could teach you to be much better behaved and never swear – not that I've ever understood why certain sounds and thoughts should be considered no-noes, but that's the way we are. I could have you saying "Please" and "Thank you", opening doors for me and not pinching girls' bums. That's a chance that nine wives out of ten would jump at, so I suppose you can comfort yourself with the thought that I'll have to stump up and face the risk that you might wake up a sex maniac or homosexual or convinced that you're a teapot or a reincarnation of Florence Nightingale.

'You know, it's lucky that you hired Paul Fletcher – quite apart from the fact that he's taken Xanthic off my hands for now. I was against your hiring Paul at the time, you may remember. He seemed to me to be just the sort of young tiger who would gather experience under your wing and then go off after real money or set up in competition, taking your best clients with him.

'But perhaps I wronged him. And perhaps I didn't. He may be sticking around because he's getting his end away with that little tart you took on as general secretarial dogsbody. They seem to have something going. I don't often go to the warehouse – why would I? – but when I have to go in I knock loudly before going through any closed doors, because I have caught them up-and-down before now. That means skirt up and zip down, in case you were wondering. I'm told that they've moved in together. If they're buying a house jointly, that may anchor him for a while.

'His moustache was coming along, by the way, but now he's started to grow a bit of a beard, so he still looks...either scruffy or fashionably unshaven, depending on your point of view.

'The only reason I give a damn whether Paul goes or stays is that he's doing a very good job, as far as anyone can see. The general opinion is that we'll be in a jam if we lose him. For a start, the staff seem ready to follow him through thick or thin. He's realizing some of the wasting assets you didn't bother about, like the last few – or few dozen – items in each discontinued line. You've paid for those, but you only stuck them on a basement shelf and forgot about them while you got on with sending out the new line. Then there were the slightly faulty ones – a stitch missing or whatever. They brought in a lady from the village who used to work with the old cobbler who had the upstairs and she's making an excellent job. I'm told that you can't see the fault after she's done her repair, not even if she points out the place to you. I'm taking one of the handbags for myself.

'In case you're thinking – in whatever kind of woolly way you manage to think, if you can think at all – that the business is suffering because of your absence, you can put it out of your mind. You have a good little team there. It never moved mountains in the past because you insisted on making all the decisions, but now – did you ever play that game in which somebody sits down and the others press down on his or her head? Then the others each put one finger under him and lift him like a feather. About thirty years ago a group of us did that with Betty Field as the subject and we threw her down the town hall steps and broke her leg. We didn't mean to; it just happened. Well, it's like that. Freed from your repressive influence, they're humming with ideas and egging each other on, but Paul and Mr Kennington together prevent them from going over the top. I'll tell you about Mr Kennington another time.

'Perhaps another reason that it works is that nobody ever told them that it's difficult. They're tackling every problem from scratch – rethinking what's possible and coming up with novel solutions. At the same time, they can recognize if something's beyond their experience and they go outside for advice. That can only be good.

'Our boys in blue don't seem to be making much progress on your case. Of course, they tell me as little as possible, but judging from the questions they're asking around the neighbourhood they know that there was a heavy-goods vehicle ahead of you on the road and the driver says that he met a car and a Telecom van travelling in the opposite direction. They haven't found the motorist but you probably saw him, because he must have passed you before your accident. I'm sure the police would love to interview you if they could. But then, if they could interview you and get intelligible answers there wouldn't be anything for them to investigate. Presumably you saw, or at least glimpsed, whoever or whatever hit you.

'Are you capable of enjoying a good laugh? Here's one for you. The police inspector, the hairy one, came to see me at the weekend. He must think that I had a hand in your accident. His questions were nearly all about our financial position – the ones that weren't about your diet and medication. Putting two and two together and then reading between the lines, they think that you may have been doped and that I was the only person who could have done it and been able to follow you as far as the crash. And we don't even have a second car. How little they know us! But perhaps they think that I doped you and then begged a lift with you. When you conked out I could have steered you to a stop before producing some sort of club. I would have had a fairly long walk home, but I could have walked over Barrow Hill with very little risk of being seen by anybody.

'You know, I'm rather enjoying our little chats. These are the first occasions that I've been able to speak to you without being contradicted or patronized. I can tell you things that you wouldn't have listened to a month ago. And I can be absolutely out-spoken. I can say the sort of cruel and vulgar things that we all long to say out loud but that I wouldn't dare to come out with if I had a conscious audience. You could say that whoever caused your accident was doing me a favour of sorts, but on the other hand I'm getting fed up of my sister's house, her company, her cats and her limited conversation. Especially her limited conversation. Frankly, and just between the two of us, I think I'm doing better, conversationally, on my own...'

Ten

The desk, usually half covered with neat stacks of letters, invoices, dockets, files and samples of leather, was almost hidden by paper patterns, some of them folded into shapes reminiscent of handbags. A smart leather handbag was acting as a paperweight. Paul straightened his back. 'We seem to be getting there,' he said. 'But we need some expert advice. I'm not saying you're not expert, Dave, but I mean *experienced* expert advice. Am I hurting your feelings?'

'It's your job to hurt feelings,' Dave said, smiling. 'It's what you do best. Anyway, my ego isn't as fragile as all that. I know I have everything except experience.'

'Excellent! I believe that the old chap who used to do leatherwork upstairs still lives in the village. Am I right?'

'I think so,' Dave said.

'Let's go and see him.'

Neither of them wanted to be seen carrying a handbag. There was a brief delay until Paul suggested that it could easily pass for a cartridge bag. Dave took that with a pinch of salt, but he carried the bag and Paul the rolled-up patterns.

It was a benign late-spring day. A few puffy clouds hung almost motionless in a dark-blue sky. The short, rough access road brought them from the yard to the end of the village street. A stout lady was working in her front garden. They had to admire her delphiniums before she was pleased to point out the home of Mr Kennington. This proved to be a small house almost indistinguishable from its neighbours except by the extreme tidiness of its garden.

They found Mr Kennington in his back garden. Very gently, he brushed a bumblebee away from his forsythia. 'Pollinate off,' he said. 'Go and attend to my apple trees.'

Paul gave a polite cough and the old gentleman stood up slowly and carefully and turned round. He was a gnome-like man, but Paul realized that part of his apparent smallness came from being bent from years of stooping over his work. When he arrived at the vertical he stood very straight with his shoulders back.

'Mr Kennington?' Paul said. 'May we have a word with you? We need a little expert advice about leatherwork.' He introduced himself and Dave.

'God bless my soul!' said the old man, and he sounded as though he meant it. 'I'm about due for a rest anyway. Come and sit down. You're from the old mill, aren't you?'

He led them to a typical picnic group of a table and two benches. The old man sank on to a bench with a groan of relief and an audible protest from his knees. 'Old joints,' he said. 'And old muscles doing work they're not used to and weren't designed for. Now, what's your problem?'

'You probably heard that Mr Merryhill's in hospital.'

'I had heard. I remember him well. We used to meet when he was setting up and I was winding down. Please send him my best wishes. Accident, wasn't it? – with that car of his?'

Paul avoided commenting one way or the other. 'He may need expensive surgery that won't be on the National Health,' he said. 'We're trying to boost the business to cover

101

the costs.' Paul laid the handbag on the table. 'We've been importing these. We're increasing our order. But Dave is a designer and he's sure that he could make a more elegant bag more cheaply. Dave, show us your patterns.'

The paper patterns were unrolled and folded in demonstration of the manufacturing stages. Paul, who had had difficulty understanding exactly what it was that Dave proposed, was surprised to find that the older man, after one or two penetrating questions, grasped every facet of the concept. Like was speaking to like.

Mr Kennington got up suddenly. 'Back in a moment,' he said. 'Prostate problem.' Walking stiffly, he entered the house.

It became a long moment. 'He's taking his time,' Dave said.

'That's how it takes them. I think we've caught his interest.'

When Mr Kennington returned it was soon obvious that his interest was indeed caught. He made one or two suggestions that Dave grasped enthusiastically. Then the old man sat back. 'It's easy to make and it'll look good,' he said. 'If I'd had a design man like you working with me, I'd still be in business.'

'Who could make it for us?' Paul asked.

'Make it for yourselves.'

'We wouldn't know where to begin – would we?' Paul asked Dave.

'Machines and leather and fastenings: I wouldn't know where to get them,' said Dave.

'Let me tell you something,' said the old man. The challenge seemed to have breathed new life into him. 'I gave up the business but it was dying on me anyway. Too much competition in areas where the designs were already set and unchangeable. There was no room at all for innovation, but the traditional products were already in overproduction. I advertised my machinery but got no replies, so I just left it there. My lease on the middle and ground floors still has a couple of years to run. You're my subtenant.'

'I didn't know that,' Paul said.

'Your Miss Jenkinson knows it all right. I can put you in touch with the best people to go to for fittings.'

'We'd appreciate that,' said Dave. 'But what about leather?'

'Some things are changing. For leather, what you want to use now is ostrich leather.

There's an ostrich farmer I know who's culling some of his flock. He reckons this bird flu could wipe him out if it comes here. And if it doesn't, the government will probably panic anyway and order a cull. So he wants his flock small enough to bring into his sheds if the flu comes close. He can sell the meat. A lot of others will be thinking along the same lines. Now would be a good time to buy the leather.'

'Is it good?' Paul asked.

'The best,' said Dave. 'Looks good. Strong. Supple.'

The old man was nodding. 'The tannery could use chrome tanning rather than vegetable tanning. As a contrast, you could use real cowhide for the straps and trims.'

Paul was still uneasy. 'I owe you a consultancy fee,' he said. 'But if we go ahead, would you come and supervise it for us? Just a few hours a day?'

The three sat silent while Mr Kennington considered. Dave was the first to speak. He could read the old man's mind. 'Suppose we put somebody in for an hour or two every day to keep your garden tidy in accordance with your instructions.'

The old man brightened. 'Now you're

talking. A garden's good to sit in. My idea of heaven is to sit in a beautiful garden and watch somebody else working in it.' Without knowing it, he was almost echoing Lynne Merryhill's words to her husband. 'To tell you the truth, I hate summer. The garden's always screaming for attention and if I try to take a comfortable seat in the house my wife chases me outside again. In winter I can take a seat and look into the fire. She can't expect me to go out and garden in the snow or pouring rain.'

'I'll join you in front of the fire when my time comes,' Dave said. 'Duke could take this bit of garden on,' he explained to Paul. 'Four or five hours a week should be enough. He isn't overworked, he's strong and he knows about gardening. He was lecturing me about how to deal with greenfly.'

'Then what you'll want,' said Mr Kennington, 'will be another couple of intelligent girls. Girls are neat-fingered and they have patience. One does the stitching while the other does the cutting-out. They keep the production line going while anybody else who's free, including myself, helps with the donkey work. You might need more if you do the dyeing in-house, but I wouldn't recommend it. Some of those chemicals are highly toxic.'

'And if it takes off?' Paul said. 'We'd only have one machine.'

'You'll be amazed how much two girls can do, once they're trained. I can see you needing another girl to fit the lining and to stand in at holiday times. If it gets too big for that team, I know where you can pick up another machine.'

They settled down to talking money. Mr Kennington was easy to deal with, neither grasping nor soft but rational and with the benefit of his years of experience behind him. He appreciated the partnership arrangement that replaced fixed wages. He broke off at one point. 'My lease has two years to run,' he said. 'By that time we can have found other premises.'

'Or a new lease?' Paul suggested.

Mr Kennington's wrinkled face pulled into an expression of distaste. 'If we can work it, well and good. But the lessor may be sticky about it. I've an idea that he wants vacant possession. If a Vernon Stokes wants to meet you, make sure that I'm present before you see him.'

Paul straightened his back. He forgot that he was sitting on a bench and began to lean back, recovering his balance with a jerk just in time. 'That's all that we need,' he said. 'If we want to renew in two years' time, the cost will have gone up. We'd better start putting money aside to pay for a move. I'll speak to Alma Jenkinson. In fact, we'd all better go and speak to Alma.'

Eleven

It had soon become clear that Julie could not be expected to act as receptionist and telephonist while sharing Paul's burdens and doing most of the typing and filing for the business. Minnie Halstead was engaged part-time to fill the gap. Minnie was a widow putting a daughter through college and so was very glad of even a modest wage coming in. She was plump but well proportioned with blonde curls and a slight squint.

Paul had been closeted with Mr Kennington, who had begged him to address him as Julian. The two men found that, despite the difference in age and experience, they had much in common. Julian Kennington was well read. His army service had shown him the world and his time in business had taught him more than mere leathercraft. They were both dusty but content after prowling the middle floor of the building, inspecting, among other equipment, a machine that looked fit to sew two tree trunks together. They had roughed out an agreement on such matters as finance and tenancy. Now Julian Kennington had retreated to familiar territory to look over his machinery while each was digesting the progress made so far.

Minnie Halstead put her head round Paul's door. There was, she said, a man very insistent on having immediate words with Paul. It was Minnie's habit to refer to any male person as a gentleman, so her use of the word 'man' was revealing. Julie looked up from her copy of the draft agreement. 'We don't want to be disturbed, do we? Who is it, Minnie?'

'It's a Mr Stokes.'

The name registered with Paul. He had been worrying about Mr Stokes. 'Julie, please let Mr Kennington know that Mr Stokes is here and ask him to join us. Come with him and take notes. Minnie, show Mr Stokes in, but not until Julian Kennington gets down here.'

Due to the various alterations made to the interior of the building over the centuries, it was necessary for Mr Kennington to go down one flight of stairs, up another, along a passage and then down a third stair before he could arrive, puffing and slightly testy, back in Paul's room. 'We'll have to open up that old doorway again,' he said.

'Stokes is here,' Paul told him.

'Ah,' said Julian with feeling. 'How do we play it?'

'Off the cuff,' said Paul.

'Right.'

Minnie introduced the visitor. He turned out to be a roly-poly man with a round, pink face and a rosebud mouth. He wore clothes that were colourful without quite going beyond the bounds of masculinity and he walked with a strut, as if he were ten feet tall and handsome with it. Paul disliked him on sight.

So too did Xanthic. The black flatcoat retriever was allowed to spend most of each day beside Paul's desk. A placid dog, usually on the lookout for food or a friend, human or canine, with whom to exchange courtesies, he had suffered a change. The hackles had risen up on his stiffly extended neck; he was up on his feet and producing a rumble so low as to be near the threshold of human hearing. Mr Stokes backed rapidly into a corner and turned pale. Paul grabbed Xanthic's collar before he could launch the threatened attack, clipped on his lead and handed him over to Minnie. His removal took all her strength but Minnie had had practice. Her daughter rode a horse.

'That is no way to greet a visitor,' Mr Stokes said. His voice was slightly shaky and his manner suggested that he was trying to put the best face on a humiliating incident.

'It's most unlike him,' said Paul. 'I can only suppose that the two of you have met before.'

Mr Stokes ignored the suggestion and bestowed an unfriendly look on Julian Kennington. 'I'd prefer to see you in private,' he told Paul.

Paul was sure that his first, instinctive reaction had been the right one. 'I dare say you would. He stays. Please sit down.'

Mr Stokes abandoned all pretence of a friendly approach. He rested his knuckles on the table and leaned across it. 'I don't need to sit down,' he said. 'You just listen.'

Paul's back was now thoroughly up – as up as it had ever been. He resented bitterly any attempt at intimidation and suspected that the mild and friendly Xanthic must have received an undeserved kick on some previous encounter. He had met men of Mr Stokes's stamp before, so he spoke quickly, before the other could continue to claim the psychological high ground. 'And I don't need anybody towering over me. *You* listen. Sit down or go. If you don't do one or the other I'll call the lads in and have you thrown out.'

'You can't talk to me like that,' Mr Stokes said. He sat down, but he leaned forward with an elbow on the desk, still miming dominance.

'Believe me,' Paul said, 'I can.'

'You may think you can. But I own this building and I want you out of here. You have a month.'

Paul looked at Julian. 'Does he?'

Julian Kennington nodded slowly. He waited for a dramatic second before adding, 'But I have a lease.'

'Not transferable.' Stokes looked smug, as though he had just played the ace of trumps.

'He isn't transferring it,' Paul said. 'He's a partner. We were just settling the terms when you arrived.'

'We'll see what my lawyer says about that.'

'We certainly will.' Julian smiled grimly.

'Miss Watts can read out the terms of the draft partnership agreement if you're in any doubt,' he said. 'Your lawyer was as sick as a parrot when we put in the time clause. It says that you cannot break the lease without giving two years' notice because of the disruption to my business. You weren't any too pleased, but the building was half-empty at the time. The empty half was earning you nothing and you were desperate to get it tenanted.'

Stokes looked as though he had bitten into a bad grape, so Paul judged that what Julian was saying so far had struck home.

Julian resumed in conversational tone. 'I'd been trained originally as a leather worker, so when I came out of the army years later it was the only other trade I knew. It had taken me long enough to find premises that suited me and I was damned if I was going to put myself in a position where I could be forced to relocate in a hurry. Both lawyers agreed that you wouldn't be able to break my lease so long as I stayed within the terms of the contract.' His gnome-like face was serious, but when Paul came to know him better he came to recognize the curl at the corner of the mouth, the flared nostril and the gleam in his eye that said that Julian Kennington was enjoying a bit of mischief, twisting the tail of somebody he disliked.

'You retired quickly enough when it suited you,' Stokes said hotly.

'I took a rest while I thought about the future. When I came to think about it, I realized that I needed some younger partners to do the rough-and-tumble part of the work and to see off prats like you. Now I'm warming up again.'

'But, just as a matter of interest, why do you want us out?' Paul demanded. 'Have we not been ideal lessees? If not, tell me how.'

For a moment Stokes looked uncomfortable. 'I have a better use for the building. Don't ask me what it is, because it's a secret. A pal of mine has spotted a niche in the market.'

'I wouldn't dream of asking you what it is because I don't give a fart,' said Paul. As soon as he could be confident that Stokes's guns were spiked he had begun, like Julian Kennington, to enjoy himself. The unwritten rule may frown on kicking a man when he's down, but that rule may not apply when the man is still struggling and does not even realize that he is down. 'We have no intention of moving, and that's that.' He was not usually filled with contrariness, but Stokes had brought out the worst in him.

Stokes abandoned the attack and returned to his conciliatory manner. 'Suppose I made it worth your while? I could find you something better.'

'Where?'

'Oh no! I'm not saying where until you've agreed to go – in writing.'

Paul and Julian sneered in unison. 'I may be young and innocent,' Paul said, 'an original babe in the wood, but my partner Mr Kennington is a wily old codger.'

'That's me all right,' said Julian. 'Wily and not getting any younger. I could probably sue over the "codger", though. I believe the word derives from "cadger". If you really know "something better", why don't you take it yourself and save us the disruption and yourself the litigation? You just show us over the "something better" and we'll give it serious consideration. If we don't like it, we'll just sit tight when the two years is up and let you try to get a court to shift us. The courts hate forcing a going concern to vacate.'

Mr Stokes showed anger again. 'I'd advise

you to get out while you can,' he said.

'We *can* get out any time we feel like it,' Paul said. 'We just don't feel like it just now.'

'Life can become very difficult for people who thwart me. You could have a fire tomorrow.'

'That's a threat.' Paul leaned forward and pointed his finger like a pistol between Stokes's eyes. 'So here's another one: if we do,' he said, 'you'll have one the day after and you'll be sitting on top of it. Why won't you tell us what you want the building for?'

'He's ashamed,' said Julian. 'He's probably going to print hardcore porn.'

'Or manufacture marital aids,' Paul suggested. 'It's a rotten job but somebody has to do it.'

For some minutes, Stokes alternated bluster with guile, but Paul and Julian had found a surprising knack of working as a team. They needled him mercilessly. In the end, Stokes jumped to his feet. 'You think you're bloody funny, don't you?'

The old man and the younger one exchanged a glance. 'Yes,' said the new partners. Julie uttered a trill of laughter. 'So do I,' she said.

When Mr Stokes, without waiting to be

shown out, had quit the building, Paul found that he had to tell his neck muscles to relax.

Julian said, 'He didn't have to say what he wants it for. He'd told us.'

'What?'

'You wait and see if I'm not right.'

'Whether you're right or wrong about that,' said Paul, 'I'm damn glad you were here when he came. He might have bluffed me into giving up the lease. From now on, we make sure that we know who's going to be the last person out and that he or she knows it too and knows how to make it all lockfast. I'll have a word with Ernest Hendry about mutual awareness.'

'His foreman lives in that cottage looking along the car park,' said Julie.

'Better and better. And I think that we might get an electrician to check the wiring. If by any chance we did have a fire, I'd like to be able to prove that we'd taken all possible care. Julie, I think we might appoint Duke our Fire Safety Officer.'

'I'll brief him in the morning. He'd better go to the fire station and meet the fire-prevention officer.'

Paul decided that a word of caution was

due. 'That's good, but tell him not to go overboard,' he said. 'If he goes for every suggestion the FPO makes, Mr Merryhill may have to wait ten years for his operation. Tell him fire extinguishers, yes; hose reels, maybe; fire escapes, no way or he pays for them himself.'

Twelve

Inspector 'Jerry' Mills was holding a briefing meeting of his small team. This had shrunk to a mere half-dozen as the Powers That Were lost faith in the chance of a successful and statistically significant result.

'So that's how it stands,' he said gloomily in his bass rumble. 'The bosses want us to wind it up. We're going to have to take part in the next sizeable case that comes in and they'll settle for an accidental death in this one. After that, nobody will say anything; but it'll be remembered. We'll have failed. What makes it worse is that this isn't murder – not yet. It's attempted murder. That's what's worse.'

A constable with a protruding Adam's apple raised a hand. 'How can that be worse?'

'Because, Symes, the killer didn't succeed. That means he may try again – and succeed.

119

And we'll be blamed because we didn't pin it on him first time around. What sticks in my gullet is that you know and I know that it was no accident. Somebody's walking around out there who attempted a murder. He may have killed before and he may intend to kill again and I don't like it one damn bit.

'We can have one more good look at this one. Like I said, you know and I know that it wasn't an accident. I'd be as happy as the next man to find a rock with blood and hair on it that had been thrown up from between the double back tyres of some lorry, but if there was anything like that it was no bigger than a pebble and wouldn't have dented the front of his skull in. And it would have been mucky and would have left dirt in the wound. But we'll look anyway.

'I think we've got all that the Telecom driver can give us. The only other potential witness that we've found so far is the lorry driver. He's due back from Plymouth and I'm seeing him this afternoon. Meanwhile, I want each of you to think. It's always helpful to put yourself in the other man's place. You have an enemy you want to kill by whacking him on the head. He's stolen your money, insulted your mother and kicked you up the arse. The time he's vulnerable is driving on a little-used, twisting country road in a sports car with the windscreen down. How would you go about it?' He paused and looked at their faces.

None of them wanted to speak up. Gloom settled over them like a furry blanket.

'Don't be afraid to suggest something that sounds silly at first – the answer when we find it will probably sound as daft as a flat-earthist on LSD. And never mind if we've looked at it before. We may have missed something. Grant, how would you go about it?'

A constable with a badly broken nose sighed. 'I'd phone in and say that he was behaving strangely and seemed to be arm-ed. The Armed Response Unit would come and blow him away.' There were several snorts of laughter. That week an innocent man had been shot by armed officers after such a phone call and several earlier instances were being dragged up by the media.

It was a sensitive subject to any policeman with some seniority. 'Not that damn silly,' DI Mills snapped. 'Symes? What can you offer?'

The constable with the Adam's apple jumped. 'Me, sir? I'd stand in the road with something heavy and clobber him as he went by.'

The inspector nodded tolerantly but he said, 'Too many objections to that one. You'd risk being seen standing, waiting. Another vehicle could follow your victim round the corner. Your victim would see you. He could swerve away or run you down. And I'd expect a skid-mark where he braked sharply, seeing a figure in the road swinging a club.'

'I think I'd go for some sort of projectile,' said the sergeant. 'There's a tree not far from where it must have happened if he was to fetch up where he did. It forks just above the ground. Some sort of scaled up boy's catapult or a big crossbow, powered by strips cut from an old inner tube, and only a smooth rock with skin on it to tell the tale. The victim had just come out of sunshine into the shade of the trees and he was wearing Reactolite spectacles, wasn't he?'

'The broken spectacles in his lap were Reactolites,' the inspector conceded.

'They would still have been dark. So if he missed over the top first time, he probably wouldn't know what it was and he could try again next day. He'd still be there to carry away the rock.'

There was a brief delay while the inspector sorted out the pronouns. Then he nodded. 'I suppose it's worth looking at again,' he said. 'You could take a couple of men and look for signs – on the tree, especially.'

'Sir,' said the newest and youngest constable. 'Sir, I have an idea.'

'Spit it out then.' Mustn't discourage the young.

'Sir, how I'd do it would be to sling a rope from the tree to a fixed point up on the banking opposite. I'd thread the rope through something heavy like a scaffolding pole, camouflage-painted. Then I could haul it up out of harm's way when somebody else came along but lower it so that it hung level at the right height when –' He broke off. He had nearly said 'when you were coming'.

'That...' began the inspector. He was on the point of denouncing the idea as ridiculous, but then it struck him that, not only was the idea feasible, but if he decried it and it then turned out to have a basis in fact, he would look the idiot to end all idiots. 'That just could be,' he said. 'At least it would allow for him arriving on a slightly different track each day. Well done, lad. You go with the sergeant and the others and look for signs. He'd need something to make a fixed point on the banking...'

'Something like the corkscrew thing they sell dog owners for fixing the dog's lead to,' said the constable, showing keen.

'I was going to say that,' said the inspector untruthfully. 'Look for the mark where it was screwed in. Or anything else. A long tent peg would do.' He would have liked to speed them on their way with a rousing speech, but nothing occurred to him. *Once more into the breach, dear friends, once more*? No, definitely not. For one thing, they were not his dear friends and they'd better not think it.

'I've waited more than long enough for a proper word with you,' the inspector told Henry Green. 'I want a statement.'

Henry was the lorry driver. Like many of his kind, he was stout and bloody-minded. He had a flat nose with enlarged pores and a Birmingham accent. 'I bloody *gave* you a statement,' he said. He looked around the interview room as if it was overdue for decoration and a new carpet. In this, he was not far off the mark.

'You gave one of my officers about fifteen words and then bug...buzzed off abroad,' said the inspector. Henry Green looked just the sort of person to run to the Police Complaints Committee if sworn at.

'I did a run to Turin with drums of chemicals,' Henry said. 'Came back with barrels of rice, didn't I?' That was true as far as it went. The fact that more than twenty illegal immigrants had travelled behind the barrels was not mentioned. 'Some of us have to work for our livings,' he added.

That statement also was true. The inspector decided to ignore the implications. 'Tell me about that morning. Tell me what you saw on the...' He looked down at his notes and quoted the road number.

'Forgotten by now, haven't I?'

The inspector's rumble became deeper – always a sign that he was close to losing his temper. 'If you have, I'll have you producing your licence, your vehicle's licence, insurance and MOT, your tachometer readings, your cargo list and all necessary certificates, every fifty yards for the rest of your life.'

After pushing awkwardness with his natural enemies as far as he dared, Henry was prepared to be friendly. He leaned back in his hard chair and lit a half-cigarette that he produced from a pocket of his overalls. The inspector was a rabid non-smoker and if Henry had been a suspect he would have put a stop to it. But Henry was a witness – almost the only witness that he had. Inspector Mills leaned to one side to escape the worst of the smoke.

'Now, guv,' said Henry, 'no need to get stroppy. There wasn't nothing to remember. I left Briggs's yard, loaded with waste, at five past nine, so I'd have been entering that road around nine ten. Takes ten minutes, it does, near enough, so I'd have come out on to the main road around nine twenty.'

'Passing the mouth of the track to Gledd Farm at what time?'

'That where it happened?'

'Just—'

'All right, all right. Call it nine fifteen.'

'That's round about the time at which the incident must have happened,' said the inspector. 'Mr Merryhill must have been close behind you by then. You didn't see a small sports car in your mirror, with the top down and the windscreen folded flat?'

'Nothing like that.'

'The incident was reported by the driver of a British Telecom van. You must have met him just after nine fifteen. He remembers you—'

Henry had been slumped in the chair in a typical lorry driver's slouch. He sat up suddenly as if goosed. 'Here! What are you trying to pull? I met a car after Gledd Farm Road and before I met the Telecom van. They was close, as if the car had just over-taken the van on the straight bit.'

'You did?' Henry had never expected to be smiled on by a senior policeman, but he was smiled on now. 'Tell me about it.'

Henry shrugged. 'It was just a car. I didn't notice in particular.'

Detective Inspector Mills's smile faded. His hands curved into claws. He would have like to get them around Henry's throat, but that would have defeated his objective. He kept them below the level of his desk. 'Tell me what you do remember,' he said slowly and grittily.

'Bugger all.'

A sting on the pride might do the trick. 'Perhaps you don't know much about cars?'

'I know about cars. I just don't know about this one. See, it's a place where the road's become dangerous – not very wide – and I was squeezing a wide vehicle past a car. Had to follow the edge of the ditch if I wasn't going to push him over the brink and into Willow Water, didn't I?'

'And after you'd gone past, you didn't look in your mirror? But perhaps you don't use your mirrors?'

Henry was stung again, as the inspector intended. His professional competence was being questioned. 'I looked in the mirror, didn't I? I saw the back of a car. It wasn't very big or very small as cars go. It looked kind of boxy and there was a spare wheel on the back so it was a four-by-four. I wouldn't even have noticed that much if it hadn't been for the colour: black over silver. Typical! Could've been a Shogun Pinin or a Vauxhall Frontera. Could've been others, but, thinking back, the impression I got was one of them two. I couldn't begin to tell you why.'

Careful probing and study of a motoring magazine lent by a sergeant in Traffic produced no more about the car.

DI Mills changed tracks. 'What about the

driver?'

'The windscreen was reflecting the sky, so he was just a dark blob. I could hardly make out that it was a man. Or could have been a bird.'

'There was only one person?'

'Far as I can remember.' Henry frowned. 'But there was something odd about him. Or her.'

'Large or small? Black, white or khaki? Hunchbacked? Bald or hairy?'

'None of those. Listen, guv,' Henry said plaintively, 'I'm doing my best, but if I sit here and concentrate until kingdom come I'll never get it. Just let me go away and get on with my life and think about it now and again and what it was that was odd will pop into my head. That's how it always works. And I'll phone you the minute it does – promise.'

There was some sense in what Henry was saying. The man had become co-operative and it was common experience that struggling for a recollection often pushed it further away. Also, the inspector wanted his tea. 'All right,' said Detective Inspector Mills. 'See that you do. If you're abroad, you can reverse the charges.'

Thirteen

Paul was having a morning in which work seemed to flow easily and any incoming letters or emails were favourable. Problems only arrived with solutions attached. If there had ever been a tunnel, there was now light at the end of it.

His buoyant mood was dispelled by a phone call from Don Clumber. The bank manager was not his usual enthusiastic self. 'I'm coming in to see you,' he said. 'Please have your updated accounts ready with a list of all outstanding credits and debts.' He terminated the call with an abruptness that might have been normal in another banker but which he had left far behind him in his recent dealings with the Merryhill partnership.

Most of the half-hour that it would take Don Clumber to arrive Paul spent with Alma, looking over her shoulder as she brought together the latest figures and printed them out, nearly driving her mad in the process.

'There isn't anything we've forgotten, is there?' he asked.

Alma's temper was becoming short. 'If there is, I've forgotten it,' she said. 'We had the auditors in a fortnight ago and they didn't spot anything; but we don't have their written report yet. And you won't have my figures either if you don't go away and leave me to it.'

'I can take a hint,' Paul said. 'Come to my room as soon as you have a printout.'

'That wasn't a hint. It was a very positive statement.'

Paul retreated to what was now recognized as his own room. This had now been redecorated. Clever colours had been amateurishly applied, but the fresh and almost jolly new image did little for him. He paced the floor for a few minutes. Then he realized that he was agonizing over nothing. Everything was on a firm footing. He sat down and tried to relax but he soon jumped up again. Financial stability has to be generally recognized or its very existence is open to doubt.

Don Clumber arrived promptly. Xanthic rose to give him his usually hearty welcome but found himself ignored. Clumber refused any offer of refreshment. His manner seemed agitated, but he refused to open discussions until they had the figures in front of them. To Paul's great relief Alma, who kept a meticulously tidy set of figures on computer, arrived almost on the heels of the bank manager, burdened by several files and a small stack of paper.

'Now,' Paul said, 'perhaps you'll tell us what this is all about.'

Clumber only nodded, which was in contrast to his usual chatty manner. He produced a folded letter from his pocket, opened it and laid it on the desk. 'This states quite categorically that you will be unable to meet your obligations. It forecasts that you will be broke by Christmas.'

'And I can see from here,' Paul said, 'that it is unsigned. Do you, in fact, have any knowledge as to its origin?'

'None,' Clumber admitted.

'Or any suspicions?'

'Again, none. So I have no way of questioning the originator. That of itself does not necessarily mean that it's untrue. The writer

132

might merely wish to avoid repercussions. I shall have to think about this with some care. It's just that, as I haven't gone to the head office for authorization for this loan, I need to consider my position carefully. I wouldn't normally take an anonymous letter seriously, you know, but I just need to go over the figures again. If there should chance to be anything in it...'

'There isn't,' Paul said, '–not as things stand at the moment. But this is the sort of self-fulfilling prophecy that does so much damage. If that sort of rumour is spread around our suppliers – plus yourself, of course – our credit may dry up. So it comes down to believing what you want to believe. However, we had the auditor in recently. He seems satisfied. Cyrus Hawkes.'

'I know him well. A reliable man.'

'We don't have his report yet, but I'll let him know that we have no objection to his discussing our stability with you. Meanwhile, here are the figures you wanted...'

Lunch time came and went in an atmosphere of irritation and mistrust. Moira was asked to fetch sandwiches. Alma fielded some searching questions and answered them with her usual precision. Later, Don

Clumber put his pen away. 'If there's any gap in your figures,' he said, 'I can't find it.' His manner, if not his words, was apologetic.

'You've seen all there is,' Alma said.

Paul was exhausted by so much detailed concentration on the financial affairs of the firm. He had some understanding of money, but he found it hard work. He was almost afraid to blink in case he dozed off. He choked back a yawn. 'If there's a gap,' he said slowly, 'it could only be caused by one of the retailers not paying up. So far there's no sign of that and their orders are all properly confirmed and invoiced, so they wouldn't have a leg to stand on. There have not even been the usual minor complaints about tiny defects. But if you see this for what it is, an anonymous letter attempting to put us into difficulties, it would make more sense if he sent a similar letter to each of our suppliers.'

'That assumes he knows who your suppliers are,' said Clumber.

Alma and Paul exchanged a glance. 'Garry Streen,' they said in unison. Alma went on to explain. 'Garry was our one unsuccessful recruitment. He interviewed well but he then turned out to be as thick as porridge. He couldn't shake off the attitude that employers are the enemy and that cheating them is fair game. I spent hours trying to explain that cheating the firm was cheating himself and all his colleagues and that he was one of the shareholders that he so much despised, but he still had the habit of skiving off, doing as little work as he could get away with and even interfering with the work of the others. We had to let him go, by unanimous vote. He would be easily corrupted.'

'That sounds possible,' Clumber said. He picked up the original letter. 'But who would have sent this?'

'I think we have a very good idea,' said Paul. His brief tiredness was receding and his brain was beginning to buzz again. 'I believe that he and young Streen live not far apart in the village, which can't be coincidence. And you can leave me to deal with him. And, Alma – you might phone any contacts that you have among our suppliers, particularly the ostrich farmers. Find out if they've had anything similar. Ask them to let us know... Oh well, you'll know what to say if it happens.'

'I trust,' said Clumber, 'that you have no

thought of retaliating in kind?'

'Not the least idea in the world,' Paul said. 'Perish the thought.'

As soon as Don Clumber had left the building he sent word round that there would be a meeting of all staff in his room within two minutes.

Fourteen

Lynne Merryhill settled herself in the bedside chair and put her gloves carefully on the locker. 'Though,' as she remarked to her husband, 'just what a patient in High Dependency and in a coma would want to put in a locker I really don't know.' Beside the chair she placed her carrier bag containing biscuits and a flask of tea, because, as she had remarked on a previous visit, the hospital tea was more likely to put people into hospital than to help them out of it. There was also a book for when she ran out of conversation or for those occasions when Aubrey was spirited away for another scan or some treatment.

'I've had a long chat with your doctor,' she said. 'Such a nice man! Did you know that he nearly became a dentist instead? But he decided that a lifetime spent looking into people's horrible mouths was not for him, besides being very hard on the vertebrae.

He decided that he'd have more chance of conquering his dislike of blood than his aversion to bad breath.

'He says that your EEGs, or whatever they call them, are showing more signs of life – especially at times when I've been talking to you, which is nice to know. It makes all the effort and laryngitis and expense seem quite worthwhile. He says that that's often the way and that coma patients often remember more of what's been said to them during the coma than they do of the accident. So that should put an end to any talk about turning off the machine and using your parts for transplants. I expect you'll be pleased to hear that. It's supposed to be the one over-riding instinct, to cling to life, but I wonder why. If you added up the credits and debits in the average life, would the sum total of happiness be above or below the median line? Is there even some huge law saying that every life will come out average for happiness? Perhaps we each have an average expectation appropriate to ourselves so that any departures, up or down, balance out. It could be that, in a miserable, impoverished life, any relief, any break, any stroke of luck seems so marvellous that it balances.

'But do you still have emotions, Aubrey? You may hear words but do you think about them? I wonder. If I tell you a funny story, do you laugh inside? That's why I'm so blunt with you. I don't want to agonize over my choice of words and apply censorship to what I tell you, if you're not taking it in anyway. It's enough of an effort to find things to talk about for a day at a time. Some women could do it without the least effort, but I'm not quite that much of a natural chatterbox.

'He says that you're getting stronger and they're beginning to think about scheduling you for surgery. We've accepted the fact that we've got to switch from the NHS to private in order for you to have this operation as soon as possible. The super-surgeon has had a look at your scans – they sent them over the wire to Glasgow rather than pay for him to come here. He says that he can do it with a ninety per cent chance of success. Just what the other ten per cent comprises I didn't like to ask. And I didn't ask for a definition of success. I'm too afraid of the answers.

'It looks as though we'll be able to afford him. Your bank manager, Mr Clumber, has been over the figures with Paul Fletcher and he seems delighted with them, and he set an overdraft limit at a level that, frankly, I thought they only allowed if you didn't need the money anyway. I had a little word with him to see if I couldn't draw a little of it for my own purposes, but apparently Paul remains the only signatory. I shall have to start being nice to Paul. I shall be due for a little holiday between when you turn the corner and when they let you come home.

'Mr Clumber seems to be most impressed with Paul and says he has a first-class business head on his young shoulders. Paul has a neat little beard now. It makes him look older and more responsible. So when Mr Clumber got an anonymous letter to say that the firm was going to go bust, Paul was able to satisfy him that it wasn't. I didn't think that bank managers were so easily satisfied, so Paul must have been very convincing. Paul says that he knows exactly who would have written such a letter and he'll fix his wagon for him. I don't know what that means, but when Paul said it there was a look in his eye that I wouldn't want him to have if he was talking about me.

'Paul, along with Mr Kennington, has managed to get the leather workshop up and running again amazingly quickly. And that little girl Moira had been dealing with all the shops that ordered the Italian goods, so Paul let her try herself out as Sales Manager. She spent three days going round with samples. Did I tell you that they took your car into the ground floor of the Mill and Paul and Duke between them straightened out the suspension and beat out the wing? They sprayed it from aerosols and you'd hardly know that it had ever been in an accident unless you looked at it against the light. Paul says that they'll get it done properly later when funds permit; your insurers won't look at it until you can give them a statement about what happened.

'Anyway, Moira used it to get round all the buyers and she came back with a fistful of orders that made Paul clutch his head and walk around in a circle. But Mr Kennington took it quite calmly and said that they'd need two more girls, probably three. He said that the machinery could cope and that they could get more ostrich skins, but they're having to go to a bigger tannery. Paul seems to have cornered the market in ostrich skins and other manufacturers are having to come to him for them – at a price, of course.

'They advertised for girls and got a lot of answers, many of them from the village. Julie sat in with Mr Kennington on the interviews. She told me that some of the girls couldn't get their heads around the system of having set percentages of the total profit and the only wage increase coming from increased profitability. And of course the bigger the firm grows the smaller one share becomes as a percentage of the overall profit, but it still grows as the business grows. Paul said that any girl too thick to get her head around that concept wasn't bright enough for us anyway. There was that boy Garry Something among the staff. You hired him some time ago. I dare say that he could have had a high old time among those girls, young people being what they are, but he seems to have been the unsociable type. A little concupiscence needn't have bothered us as long as they did it off the premises and outside of working hours. (What was it that the lady said about doing it in the street and frightening the horses?) But he turned out to be a dud and they got rid of him anyway.

'The first orders were wanted for very quick delivery because the shops needed to be ready for the Christmas trade. I'd have thought that it was early enough for that, with Christmas still being months and months off, but apparently the shops like to get the goods in time for people to see them and go away and sell themselves on the idea that *that's* what they want for Christmas. So everybody turned to and the orders went out to the shops and they've gone down a bomb. Repeat orders are coming in and they're being asked if they can't make matching purses and wallets. Apparently the chrome-tanned ostrich leather is setting a new fashion. They're thinking about it. But there was an enquiry – from the bank manager, no less – as to whether we could do a matching briefcase – sort of his-and-hers bags; so Dave turned his mind to it and what he came up with is similar but different and somehow masculine, while the handbags are definitely feminine. Now Moira's gone off with the sample to do another tour of the buyers and Mr Kennington's phoning around to find more sources of ostrich skin.

'Are you pleased about all this? You may be happy that we can afford your operation, but you won't be enjoying the fact that Paul's doing it by driving a coach and horses through all your ultra-conservative principles. Is that gall and wormwood to you? But then, what you think may matter a lot to you, until you can communicate with us we don't know what it is and so we needn't worry too much about it even if we did. Just bear in mind that the prime motivation for all this effort is to be sure that you get the best.

'There's been one rather nasty spin-off. Part of the sales drive entailed Moira getting a schoolfriend of hers who works for a glossy magazine to interest their features editor in the handbags. "Small firm hits fashion jackpot" – that sort of thing. The publicity has brought some of the wrong kind of interest: threatening letters from the animal-rights activists. Apparently, it's borderline but almost all right to eat an ostrich, but you mustn't make use of the skins. Why that should be worse than using leather beats me, but perhaps dicky birds are more cuddly than moo-cows. But all the fuss has only brought us another level of publicity. We're getting enquiries now from all over the place. Some even from Italy, would you believe?

'Which reminds me, in a funny sort of

way: I thought that I was giving the perfect impression of a doting wife – which is what I am, if you can count a sort of love–hate relationship, because, let's face it, I've been a good wife to you, but you haven't always treated me the way a good husband should. That police inspector – the fat one with the rumbly voice and hair growing out of every visible orifice – seems to have guessed that life with you isn't a rose garden, because he came to question me again last evening. I think that the whole investigation of what happened to you is dying on its feet, because he seems to have lost most of his team and is functioning almost as a one-man band.

'His questions, this time around, had changed their slant. He spent a good twenty minutes on asking how you and I had been getting on prior to your whatever-it-was. I was adamant that we rubbed along at least as well as the average couple, which isn't saying an awful lot, but that you were sometimes rather free with your hands around the young girls – playing stinky-finger, to put it bluntly – and that some aggravated father, brother or boyfriend might have had it in for you. In the end, he asked me pointedly if that didn't sometimes make

145

me want to hit you with something heavy, though he didn't put it quite like that, and I said no – that it didn't cost me anything or lose me anything. In fact I rather thought that having an outlet like that stopped you from getting bigger ideas and leaving me for some dolly bird. So why, I asked him, should I grudge you your little bit of fun when the girls seemed to take it as a compliment? I think he was shocked but satisfied. I'd like to know what put him on to that line of questioning. One of your little girlie friends must have been talking.

'All the same, it makes one wonder again who did this to you. If we knew how, we'd probably know who. I really don't see how anybody could whack you over the head while you're driving around in that wild manner of yours. Somebody suggested knockout drops – chloral hydrate, do they call them? All I know – and this is only from reading thrillers – is that you black out suddenly and come round later with the father and mother of a headache. There are plenty of things that you take and I don't that something like that could have been added to – your medication for a start and brown demarara sugar in your morning coffee. It wouldn't need to be anything too fast-acting. Our house wasn't exactly burglar-proof – you wouldn't spend the money – but I've had security locks put on all doors and windows since then and I'm getting a price for electronic alarms. If that's how it was done – by loading something soporific into your coffee, which you always gulp down just before setting off – the culprit would have had to follow you up, of course; but there'd be no doubt that you'd either crash big-time or come more or less gently to a halt and wait there for your brains to be knocked out. With a bit of luck it might have passed off as a traffic accident. He'd have been gambling with other motorists' lives, but I suppose that anyone ruthless enough to try to kill you wouldn't boggle at that.

'I think that's all the gossip for now. I'll read to you some more, from the same book. I know that it isn't exactly your cup of tea, but I like it and we don't know whether you hate it or not. Anyway, it must relieve the boredom and you're not in much of a position to object, are you, my love?'

She began to read, but as she came to the climax of the story her voice faded away and soon she was reading quietly to herself.

Fifteen

Moira Blessed had had a crush on Paul from the moment of her interview for the job. She was not alone among her girl colleagues. Paul, after all, was a mature man, not lacking in attractiveness, and he had the added glamour of seniority equating with power. The discovery that he seemed rather firmly attached to Julie came as a blow, but she had been disappointed before in affairs of the heart and was beginning to see herself as a romantic figure, doomed to love in vain, so she had kept her crush strictly for a bedtime fantasy.

At one time it had seemed that this reticence might have been just as well. Andrew Jones had joined the workforce in place of the departed but not regretted Garry Streen. Andrew's real name was Elvis, but he had abandoned this at an early age and reverted to the middle name that had been chosen to honour not the saint but Mr Lloyd Webber, another of Mrs Jones's heroes.

Andrew was no Adonis, but he was well above average among Moira's small circle. He had pale hair, almost but not quite blond. His features were regular, standard issue rather than outstanding, but he had very blue eyes. It was his voice that Moira found attractive. On the death of his parents, he had been brought up by an aunt who had married beneath her. Andrew had thus acquired an accent that could have passed anywhere. Before having even set eyes on him but on hearing his voice on the phone, Moira had determinedly transferred part of her romantic aspirations to him. She was well aware that she was settling for second best, but that, she thought, was going to be the story of her life. That Andrew turned out to have a natural talent for leatherwork was a bonus. This, however, was totally outweighed by the fact that he seemed unaware of her existence.

Alma Jenkinson had become a mother figure to Moira and it was to Alma that she turned in her time of trouble. 'I don't know how to make him notice me,' she said plaintively. 'Andrew has the other girls around him all day.'

'Andrew? I thought it was Paul who filled your dreams.'

Moira turned pink. She had thought that her crush on Paul was her own tender secret. 'Andrew,' she said. 'But...'

'But...?'

It came in a rush. 'I do fancy Mr Fletcher, but he'll never be available. I can see my life stretching ahead like a dismal swamp with never a trace of romance. I do want a boyfriend, somebody who fancies me, and Andrew's the best I know. He's nice-looking and his voice sends a little thrill up my back.'

Alma could sympathize. 'Not one of those girls is prettier than you,' she said.

'If that's true, it still doesn't help,' Moira said with a catch in her voice. 'He doesn't notice. By the time he does, he'll be hooked up with one of them.'

Alma sighed. What a lot these teenagers didn't know. Moira had lost her mother early and, like Andrew, had been reared by an aunt. But apparently her aunt had been more interested in conveying information about domestic economy than about the birds and bees. Moira had reached eighteen or nineteen in a state of blinkered ignorance, which an acute personal shyness might well turn into a permanency. Alma herself had been shaped by a similar shyness. As a girl, she had been attractive enough, but she had never managed to keep a steady boyfriend at first. In her anxiety to be accepted she had let it be seen that she was not unwilling to share a bed or even, at a pinch, a bale of straw or a grassy bank. Thereafter, she had never been without male company for long, but she had never married. On the whole she did not feel that life had cheated her. She had had about as much sex as the average wife and, if there was nobody to support her, at least she need answer to nobody.

She considered Moira until the girl fidgeted under her scrutiny. 'For a start,' Alma said, 'you've got to look like a sexy female. He sees you mostly in those shapeless trousers and your coat or a sweater. You look like a boy. The weather's warm. Do you have any skirts?'

'Well yes, but—'

'Wear them. And perhaps show a bit of cleavage every so often. And wear more make-up.'

Moira was showing signs of confusion. 'But I've been getting on all right in business. I've brought in the orders. I can't be that hideous.'

Alma looked round, but they were in her cubicle, which, though small, was nearly soundproof. 'Hideous is different and how you look's got nothing to do with how good you are at your job. You've been looking businesslike. If you'll settle for businesslike, you're already there. Not many men, and no young men, want just plain businesslike. You need to add in a bit of sexy, too.'

Moira's eyebrows went up and her mouth made a kissable 'Ooh' of surprise. She was a girl and young. She had thought that that made her sexy enough by definition. 'How?' she asked.

'Your next pay packet should be the first of the good ones. Shake out your ponytail and spend some of it at a good hair stylist. Go to a make-up adviser in a big store.' Alma thought back. Her own years as a man-trap were not so far behind her. 'Then learn to walk the walk. Once he notices you as a sexy female, you can begin to flirt a little. Make him laugh. Give him a secret smile. Lower your eyes. This is when you can let your shyness work for you. But keep reminding him that you're a woman. Let's see you walk sexy.'

Alma had to pull her feet back as Moira tried to walk sexily in the small space available. 'That's not sexy,' she said. 'That's more like humble. Sway sinuously.'

Moira tried again.

'Do you feel sexy?'

Moira thought about it. 'I don't know what sexy feels like,' she said at last.

'To look sexy you've got to feel sexy.'

'But I don't know how.'

Alma thought back and mustered her arguments. 'When you walk, you've got to feel mean and dangerous. Men always want what they can't have. Let the boy think that you might fend him off but that you might make a grab at him. And to do that you've got to feel that you could. Try going out without knickers on. Not in a strong wind, of course. You'll find that the feeling that you know something important and wicked and sexy that they don't know brings a sense of power. The walk will come.'

'In a skirt?'

'Of course in a skirt.'

Moira thought it over. 'I don't see what difference that would make if I'm wearing tights.'

Alma closed her eyes for a minute. This was like trying to teach a camel to waltz. On the other hand, the girl was right. 'Don't wear tights. You're supposed to be living dangerously. Show me your legs. One will do.' Obediently Moira pulled up a trouser turn-up. 'White and pasty. You need nylons. Do you have a suspender belt?'

Moira, dumbly, shook her head. 'I could get hold-ups.'

Alma recalled that the world was changing. 'You really can't trust those things and there's something not quite dignified in having to pull them up even if that does attract male eyes. You might have difficulty buying the right sort of thing locally. I can provide you with something. Come to my house this evening.' Alma had plenty of the 'right sort of thing', carefully wrapped in tissue paper in her bottom drawer. She had never expected to have recourse to any of it again though she could not bear to part with it because of sentimental associations – the associated memories she hoped to toy with during her old age. Now she rather liked the idea of her prettier accoutrements having a fresh chance to work their magic.

Alma was a sentimental soul but, like Julie, she had never let sentiment cloud her appreciation of sex. There were, however, certain caveats that a mother-substitute should offer to a maturing girl. In dispensing quite such fundamental wisdom she might be unleashing a new force on an unsuspecting world. 'You probably don't intend to go "all the way",' she suggested.

Moira shook her head, looking shocked. It had been drilled into her that nice girls did not go 'all the way'. Never. Girls who did were beyond the pale and doomed to a life of sin and a place in hell. Nevertheless, what little she knew about the procedure, while frightening, had a certain allure.

'All the same,' said Alma, 'once you go a bit of the way you'll want to go the rest. That's what the devil gave you hormones for. Rule one is...don't! You have a very difficult tightrope to walk. Keep the boy interested, but "going all the way" probably won't do that. Once he's got what he wanted, he may lose interest. But you won't obey rule one for ever. People don't. Hot young blood takes over. Listen to me for a minute and I'll tell you rule two, which is how to comport yourself so as to please the man but keep him in his place; and remember: "safe sex".'

Moira nodded her head slowly as if she vaguely recalled a biology lesson at school that had broached the subject.

Alma was not reassured by Moira's expression and silently regretted ever having got involved.

Sixteen

Paul had no very high opinion of the intelligence of Mr Stokes. It came as no surprise to him, therefore, when Stokes arrived at the office in a thundering temper but without an appointment. Paul received him graciously in the office. Mr Stokes refused coffee.

'Please sit down,' Paul said.

Mr Stokes had no wish to sit down, but nor did he want to get into another argument on the subject. He sat. 'This is your doing,' he said.

'Something seems to be troubling you,' Paul said. 'Tell me about it.'

'You know damn well,' Stokes burst out.

Paul did indeed know, and probably in more detail than Mr Stokes did, but it was necessary for him to pretend total ignorance. If Stokes had any sense, which Paul doubted, he would be wired up with a recording device. So Paul merely looked a question.

'Why don't you admit that you were behind it?' Stokes demanded.

'Why don't you admit that you sent anonymous letters to my bank manager and others? Tell me what you're talking about.'

Stokes wisely avoided answering the first question. 'Yesterday afternoon,' he ground out, 'I was in the town. I visited the bank in Denbeigh Street just before it closed. When I came out, the schools were letting out and the street was crowded with children.'

'As usual?'

'As usual,' Stokes said without thinking.

'You make a habit of banking there just as the schools come out?'

Stokes's complexion went from pink to dusky red and his voice climbed the scale. 'Yes... No... There's no connection. What are you suggesting?'

'I only asked. So what happened?'

Stokes's brows came down, giving him the look of a sulky child. 'You were hinting at some kind of voyeuristic interest in school-children. And you know damn well what happened. Some damn girl who looked about twelve punched me in the stomach and shouted that I'd put my hand up her skirt and felt her bottom.'

'Well, if you will do that sort of—'

'You know bloody well that I didn't do any such thing.' Stokes's voice had gone up into a yelp and Paul thought that it was only his scowl that prevented his eyes from popping out altogether. 'But one or two other voices cried out that they'd seen it. That means it must have been a put-up job. A conspiracy.

'I was so flabbergasted that I froze for a moment. An angry mob gathered round. I protested that I hadn't done that or anything like it, but nobody listened. Things were getting nasty. I was even happy when a policeman made an appearance, more fool me! By then there was no sign of the original child or of any of the ones who'd said that they saw the incident.'

'There you are, then,' said Paul. 'No evidence. It seems that you'll get away with it.'

Stokes seemed to be on the verge of a stroke. 'There was nothing to get away with,' he said shrilly. 'I hadn't done anything. How often do I have to tell you? But in any crowd you get busybodies. You get people who push themselves forward to gain attention. You get people who listen to a story and convince themselves that they saw it all, and others who bear false witness because they think that somebody guilty is, like you said, getting away with something. Several people told the policemen that they'd seen it, but then they melted away. It ended up with a fat old woman, the type that sits in judgement on everyone else and always has to be in the right, saying she'd seen it all and it was a disgrace – nice young girls being molested by paedophile abusers. That got the bystanders going again.

'I was taken, almost dragged, to the police station. They searched me and produced a small pornographic magazine from one of my pockets although I'd never seen it before; somebody must have slipped it in there quite deliberately during all the fuss and flap, which goes even further to show that it was a conspiracy and not just a case of mistaken identity. By that time there was another putative eyewitness and I had to wait – in a cell – while statements were taken. If the two stuck to what they'd been saying earlier, their statements disagreed with each other, but nobody seemed to mind that.

'I never did manage to reach my solicitor

– I have an appointment with him later this morning – but eventually they warned me that charges would probably follow and they bailed me.'

Paul pulled his lower lip. 'You'd better ask your solicitor about the Sex Offenders' Register.' He had very little idea what he was talking about, but he made it sound convincing. 'Once you're on that, if any further accusations arise, the burden of proof is on you and it can be very difficult to prove that you didn't do something. It seems to me that you have a real problem.'

Mr Stokes still looked ready to burst, but he was holding himself together by sheer effort of will. 'You can call these people off,' he said in a choked voice. 'If you do, I'll extend your lease indefinitely.'

Paul looked at him as blankly as he could manage. No doubt Mr Stokes's solicitor would put him straight in the morning. Paul was tempted to get something in writing, but the complications might be endless. 'I don't know why you think that I can do anything about your troubles,' he said, 'but I'll do what I can, if you write to my bank manager and anybody else who received your anonymous letters, stating that there was no truth in your earlier communication – and signing your own name.'

'But I can't do that,' Stokes said. His eyes were popping. 'That would be confessing...'

Paul knew that he could never push Stokes as far as that, but before settling along the lines suggested by the other he would give him a few sleepless nights. 'To writing anonymous letters? Exactly,' he said. 'But until you do that I won't move a finger to help you. What I will do is to point out to you what should be obvious to you – that this firm employs a number of young girls whose jobs were put in jeopardy by untruthful anonymous letters; and each has sisters and cousins and friends. I suggest that you remember that and walk very gently from now on.'

Paul was tempted to go on rubbing the other's nose in the mess, but on consideration he decided that pontificating was not quite his style. He watched coldly as Stokes got to his feet and stumbled out of the room.

Seventeen

'So you're scheduled for surgery at last,' Lynne Merryhill said. 'Well, I suppose it's a step forward. But they've warned me not to expect you to open your eyes and immediately be your old self – not that you ever were a chatterbox. My first thought was that there were certain parts of your old self that we could well leave behind. Unfortunately those are the parts I suspect you're hanging on to so far and I doubt if the surgeon would be willing to do anything selective about it. Just don't think that I haven't noticed that you sometimes get an erection when I tell you what your younger workers get up to. Alma keeps me posted. I just hope their mothers never find out. Alma and I sometimes have a chat on the phone in the late evenings.

'So you're taking some of it in. Well, at least I can be assured that you're paying attention, so I must be getting through to you on some level. I wonder if you have enough consciousness to enjoy it.'

There was a long pause while she gave some thought to that question. She dug into her bag for some knitting. She found that her thoughts flowed more freely when she had something to occupy her hands. She resumed more briskly.

'Everything seems to be going swimmingly with the business. If there are hiccups they haven't been telling me. Of course, there's no denying that they've been lucky. They're scrambling now to get the new briefcases out in time for the Christmas trade, but it's amazing how much a small but well-organized production line can turn out, working eight hours plus a day and with the prospect of a share of the profit. They don't get an increased rate for overtime but the more and the faster they work the better the money. They tried to get me to come in and help with the marking of the hides, would you believe? I had to point out that I spend most of my days in here and the rest of my time trying to catch up with everything else.

'With no middleman to skim off the cream, the figures look good. In fact, in some respects we *are* the middleman.

'And the brother-in-law of the policeman in charge of your case came up with a proposition. He has a small plastics factory, only a mile or two from ours, mostly making pharmaceutical hardware – brushes and bottles and things like that. He'd quarrelled irreparably with the wholesaler who'd been handling his stuff and had tried to rip him off, so he said. He decided to do his own advertising and fliers and he wanted to know if Paul could take on the packing, distribution, invoicing and so on for him.

'Paul was inclined to go for it. There's no shortage of warehouse space and he liked some of the products. In particular there's a bath brush with a feature for getting in between the toes, which should appeal to the older person who can't get down there so easily any more. They make almost everything you'd need to put in a toilet bag as a Christmas present, except for a nail file and tweezers that they could get Ernest Hendry to make, and Dave already has a brilliant idea for the bag. Paul drove a good bargain. You'll need a new toilet bag when you start getting around again. I think I'll get you one for Christmas. Allowing for the need for a new van, the discounted cash-flow forecast looks as though they'll have very little need for the overdraft facility, even after paying for your operation.

'It isn't all plain sailing, though. Among the workers was that boy Garry something. Alma says that she couldn't have faulted him in interview – he seemed intelligent and energetic. After the partnership was formed it turned out that he didn't see why he should work hard for "the bosses". He seemed to imagine some amorphous "they" lurking in a gilded stock exchange and getting fat on his labours. He spent much of his time reading and smoking in the toilet. He just couldn't get hold of the idea that he was stealing from himself and his fellow workers as well as risking burning the place down. He got one written warning and then they gave him the push by unanimous decision. That was democracy working the way it should, not the way it usually does. The procedure may not have been legal but I don't suppose that he'd even heard of a tribunal. I think I told you that already, but you know it's very difficult to think of new things to say.

'As I said before, we've been having problems with the animal-rights fanatics. They started picketing the place because of the ostrich leather. After a couple of days they brought along a photographer and some reporters. Paul had seen it coming and he went out and faced down the leader. He asked him, in front of the reporters, if he ever ate meat. The man said that he didn't. Paul produced a photograph of him eating a hamburger and asked him whether he really thought that if a creature was killed for food it was morally desirable to waste its hide. I will say that Paul was very good. And he looked very well in the photographs the reporters took. His beard has filled in a bit and they're getting the knack of trimming, almost sculpting, it to suit his features.

'It all sort of evaporated after that incident, but I understand that the police have interviewed that man about your accident. If people can get so heated up about breeding hamsters for research that they'll snatch a body out of a grave, they might well decide to knock the proprietor of a leather business on the head. But he seems to have come up smelling of roses. Apparently he and his disciples were at the other end of the country at the time, protesting about cruelty to silkworms or something.'

She fell silent for several minutes while she turned a heel. 'I'm making you bedsocks. Your feet always did tend to get cold. What else...? Paul has carried on with your training of Xanthic. I lent him your copy of Peter Moxon's book. He phoned up and wanted to know if it would be all right if he entered Xanthic in retrieving tests. I said to go ahead.

'That's about all the news. I gather that they've got an extended lease from that man Stokes and at a bargain price. Whenever the subject comes up there's a sort of tremor of amusement runs around the assembled staff, but nobody will explain. Then there's some friction between Paul and Julie; perhaps they're working too hard. Otherwise everything's rolling along smoothly. They're all much too busy to *do* anything. I may not be in again tomorrow; I have a man coming in about the hall carpet. If you're thinking in there, I've given you plenty to think about to pass the time. If not, it can't matter very much.'

Eighteen

Detective Inspector Mills did his chances of further promotion no good at all when he expressed a magnificent disinterest in how the statistics looked. He had shocked his superintendent by commenting that nothing could lie like statistics, but he stood by that opinion. What counted, he insisted, was results, not numbers; and if that view counted against him in the promotions race, so be it. Statistics only led to a rush to clear up the easy cases. Some of his superiors secretly agreed with him. Inspector Mills usually got better-than-average results, so he was tolerated. His ambitions were aimed at success rather than promoting himself out of what he did well. Thus everyone was satisfied.

Adhering to his own principles, he refused to have the file closed on the case of Aubrey Merryhill. It was, he insisted, not a freak accident but a case of attempted murder.

Mr Merryhill, unfortunately, had not been so helpful as to regain consciousness and confirm his opinion, but DI Mills was allowed to continue his enquiries provided that they did not hinder any other case in hand. Thus, on a day when he was waiting for the result of an autopsy and also for a burglar, caught red-handed, to decide whether or not he was going to confess and save several weeks of patient gathering of evidence, he found himself with sufficient leisure to look again at the case that still tantalized him. He phoned Henry Green's employer.

Henry, complete with lorry, met the inspector at the Briggs's Yard end of Gledd Road (so called locally because, although it occasionally served as a short cut between places of little importance, it had once been the principal approach to Gledd Farm). The lorry was parked on the only piece of soft verge, which might have infuriated the local authority but meant nothing to DI Mills. Henry was about to lower himself to the ground, but the inspector forestalled him by clambering clumsily up into the passenger's seat.

'Take me along Gledd Road,' he said.

Henry was pleased to be facetious. 'If it's a taxi you want—' he began.

The inspector's deep voice dropped another tone – always a danger sign. 'If I wanted a taxi, I'd call one. What I want is none of your lip but for you to drive me the way you went that day, telling me what you saw and heard and thought and did. Maybe that'll refresh your memory and maybe it won't, but at least I'll get to see the scene as you saw it. Your boss approves. Get going before I charge you with causing an obstruction.'

Henry, failing to think of a suitably witty riposte, got going. The panda car that had brought the inspector fell in behind. After a minute, DI Mills had to slow Henry down so that he could assimilate the whole view and seek out any nuances. At first, the road ran more or less level between fields. As the ground rose on the left it fell on the right until they were running along the side of a small, shallow valley, close to the bottom. The bottom was marked by a tumbling stream that, as they progressed, cut deeper into the valley bottom. The trees encroached so that the sunlight flickered uncertainly, the fields vanished and soon the road was perched above the stream. There were occasional warning posts and stretches of Armco safety barrier.

'Where did the MG overtake you?' Mills asked.

'Here, you trying to trick me?' Henry said. 'It didn't. Tell you summink else, though. It's come back to me with thinking about it. Or am I imagining things?'

The DI's spirits dropped. Only too often a witness who goes over and over events in his mind will begin to graft in imagined variants. 'Just tell me what you think you saw,' he said.

'I think I saw a flash, like the sun was reflecting off another vehicle catching me up. I thought for a moment somebody was giving me a flash of his headlamps and then I realized he wasn't.'

'His windscreen was folded flat.'

'It'd have to be,' Henry pointed out. 'The sun was behind him. About here it was.'

The inspector made no reply, but he noted the implication that the MG had been almost on the lorry's tail. 'Tell me where you met the car and the Telecom van. Henry,' said DI Mills, 'you're looking puzzled.'

'There was something else,' Henry said. 'Can't think what. This is about where I met the car. The Telecom van was just behind; I think the car had just overtaken it.'

'That agrees with what the Telecom driver told us, but he had even less idea about the car than you had.'

Henry activated his hazard-warning flashers, pulled in towards the side and stopped, blocking the road to the passage of anything wider than a motorbike and sidecar. 'Listen, guv,' he said, 'if it's right that the Telecom van driver reported the accident or whatever...'

'It is.'

'Well, I don't see it. The MG came to a stop about here?'

'Just a few yards further on.'

'I can't see him – Mr Merryhill – being hit after I'd passed the Telecom van and before he arrived where you say he was stopped. It was an empty road and there wasn't *time*. The car would have seen him first.'

Mills filed the words away in the hope of extracting a meaning from them when he had more leisure. 'Henry,' he said sternly, 'what was the "something else"?'

'I got it!' Henry shouted.

'Tell me, then. Come on, man. What was the "something else"?'

'No, not that,' Henry said. 'The other thing.' The detective inspector was still struggling to interpret his ramblings when Henry went on. 'The car.'

'What about it?'

Being helpful to the police fell outside Henry's normal patterns of behaviour, but having once started he found it easier to go on. 'I couldn't make out the driver, but I could see the dark shape where he was. It was a left-hand drive. See, I was too concerned watching the road and the verge to take a good look at it as it went by. I really only saw it in my mirror from behind. The side the driver was sitting and the way the spare wheel was mounted should have looked wrong way round and they didn't; that's why I didn't notice enough to remember. See what I mean?'

Inspector Mills spent only a second trying to visualize a left-hand-drive ORV seen in a mirror. The fact remained that the car had a left-hand drive – which meant that of the two makes suggested by Henry, the Shogun was much the more likely. Anybody who had spent time abroad might well have brought back a Japanese car; but a Briton, even a Briton serving a short-term contract

174

abroad, would be more likely to settle for a right-hand-drive Vauxhall, if he did not already possess such a vehicle. 'At least you're starting to think about it. And what was the "other thing"?' he asked.

'Gimme a minute.'

Henry engaged a low gear. The lorry pulled forward slowly on a sudden uphill gradient. 'It must have happened about here,' Mills said.

Henry drove on for fifty yards or so. They passed the old road to Gledd Farm – no more than a track passing over an obviously ancient and narrow bridge shaded by the surrounding trees. The stonework was mossy but seemed to be in adequate repair. It looked pleasantly cool compared to the heat building up in the lorry's cab. 'There was somebody here,' Henry said. 'On the bridge. Seemed to be waiting. *That's* what it was.'

'But Mr Merryhill never reached here. His car stopped near where we stopped just now.'

'Can't help that, guv. I only saw him out of the corner of my eye, but it was a man and not a shadow. I'm telling it like it was. That's what you want, isn't it?'

Detective Inspector Mills wanted to be given facts that slotted into some coherent theory and without running contrary to each other, so he remained silent. When they arrived at the main road he had Henry pull up. To Henry's surprise, he thanked him for his help before transferring to the panda car with some relief.

After Henry's lorry, the police car seemed luxuriously smooth and quiet. He returned to his office, where he started drawing maps and diagrams, rendering himself more confused than before. It was almost a relief when the burglar decided to plead not guilty and his workload returned to normal. He could put Aubrey Merryhill on the back burner with a clear conscience while he embarked on an orgy of identity parades, statement-taking and dragging out of various laboratories the results of fingerprint photography, DNA tests and the analysis of innumerable dust samples.

Nineteen

In common with most of the partners (formerly employees), Alma lived in the village and could easily pop home for lunch. She returned one day to find Moira sheltering in her tiny office. Moira was clearly woebegone and it was her habit when depressed to seek sanctuary with Alma. 'Oh dear!' Alma said. 'Do I gather that you're still without benefit of a boyfriend?'

The query was kindly meant but it triggered a fresh trickle of tears. Alma proffered a box of tissues and Moira blew her nose loudly.

'I've done everything you said. I thought it was going to work. I do feel different.'

'Sexier?'

'Yes. And colder.' She gave a little snort of self-deprecating laughter. 'I was beginning to wonder how anybody could resist me.'

'But Andrew managed it?'

'He's making out with Jessie. I found them in the paper store. You wouldn't believe what they were doing.'

'I think I would.' Alma thought that at least half of Moira's indignation was because she knew so little about the subject. The other half was because neither Andrew nor anybody else was doing it with her. 'Never mind. There are plenty more fish in the sea.'

Moira shook her head. 'I can't be bothered with men. I think they're stupid,' she said.

'They are,' Alma said, 'but they're nice to have around.'

'If you do have them around,' Moira said miserably. She started sniffing again.

'Persevere,' Alma said. 'Some day the sun will shine.'

Xanthic had tucked himself away below the desk. He was keeping a low profile. He knew that he was under discussion and that the comments were not wholly favourable.

'Either that dog goes or I go,' Julie said. 'He farts and scratches and leaves hairs all over the carpets.'

'Yellow hairs would be worse. He's a whole lot better since I changed his diet,' said Paul.

'He farts less and he's stopped scratching, but the hairs are as bad.'

'If I got a little help with brushing and bathing...'

'You're not getting the point,' Julie snapped. 'I don't want to do a lot of work so that you can hang on to a dog that isn't yours and that I don't even like. Put him into kennels or get Mrs Merryhill to take him with her, or abandon him on the side of the motorway for all I care; I don't want him in my house.'

Although she was resorting to her favourite means of persuasion and showing a lot of very pretty leg, Paul decided that he was getting rather tired of Julie. Thank God he hadn't married the girl! She was marvellous in bed and always game for a romp between the sheets or anywhere else; but although she used a lot of words, she had very little to say, so that he found sustaining a conversation with her to be hard work. And he was astonished to realize it, but you could get rather tired of sex. There seemed to be one or two misapprehensions to be cleared up. 'It isn't your house; it's my house,' he pointed out gently.

Julie drew herself up and turned red. 'It's our house.'

'It's our home,' Paul said. 'But the house is in my name. I bought it with my own money and I don't recall you putting up a single penny to help with any of the running costs.'

Julie's eyes narrowed. Conversely, her nostrils flared. 'Is this your way of saying that if you have to choose between the dog and me, the dog wins?'

Paul considered. It was beginning to look as though life with Julie would mean an eternity without dogs. He had rather been looking forward to having at least one dog of his own. His time with Xanthic had been an eye-opener. He was discovering, as had so many men before him, the benefit of a silent companion offering unconditional devotion. 'I hadn't meant it that way,' he said. 'But I don't intend to kick Xanthic out.'

'Couldn't you keep him in the garage or something? – build a kennel in the garden?'

Paul kept his temper, but it was obvious that there was no middle ground. 'I could, but I won't do it. He's used to being in the house and he wouldn't understand. He'd pine. I'm not going to put either of you out.'

Julie's face looked pinched and the colour

had drained so that it was now blotched white. Paul wondered where the attractive siren had gone. 'I'll move my things out straight away,' she said.

Paul sighed. Trust a woman to make a drama out of a change of domestic arrangements. 'If you have somewhere else to go, all right. But you don't have to rush it. Just – if you take up with somebody else, don't bring him to my house. All right?'

They looked at each other. Julie looked even less attractive. Paul got ready to duck if she started throwing things, but he knew her throwing was so inaccurate that he would be in danger of ducking into instead of away from the trajectory. Suddenly she said, 'All *right!*'

Whatever her failings as a companion, she was good as a colleague. 'I hope that we can still work together,' he said. 'I value you.'

'You're a louse,' she said, 'but you're a damn good businessman and you're doing well for all of us. You can count on me.'

Paul nodded. He thought that a few weeks, even a year or two, of celibacy would be quite acceptable. He intended to sleep and sleep.

Only the next day Moira appeared suddenly in his office doorway. Paul had already noticed that she had been looking very pretty lately, more like a girl, and she was walking as though she knew it. She usually resembled a rather scruffy boy, but his mind had been too fully occupied to register the change. That her eyes were puffy from tears quite passed him by.

'Mr Kennington asked me to fetch you,' Moira said. 'They've sent the wrong catches, but they're slightly cheaper and just as good and he wants to know if you think they'll do.'

They set off up the stairs. Moira, in the lead, modestly gathered the hem of her skirt at her knees. At the top, she stopped, turned and picked a tray of gilt fittings off a worktop. 'I've to show you this,' she said. 'These are what came.'

At that moment somebody on the ground floor opened one of the big doors. This unfortunately coincided with a sudden gust of wind across the car park that flung the door open and found its way up the stair. Moira, sparing one hand for a desperate grab at the hem of her skirt, handed him the tray of disputed samples. She would have turned to flee, but he had hold of her arm.

The samples went tinkling down the stair.

Later, she found Alma in her cubicle. Moira closed the door and leaned back against it. She closed her eyes, hoping that the world would go away. The world, however, had no intention of doing any such thing. She began to wonder which would be the least painful method of suicide.

'What on earth's the matter?' Alma asked. 'You've gone white. You look like an albino prune.'

Moira found her voice. 'Alma, it's awful. It's terrible. I can't think of anything worse.'

'You could if you tried. Sit down, take it easy and tell me what happened.'

Moira slumped into the visitor's hard chair and put her face in her hands. Her voice was consequently muffled. 'If somebody was to tell me that the world was coming to an end, I'd just say, "Good!". I was taking Mr Fletcher up to the first floor to show him the sample catches that came in and just as I turned round somebody opened the door downstairs and there was a whoosh of wind and...and...'

Alma caught on immediately. 'And you're still not...'

Moira shook her head. 'No.' She looked

up, piteously.

With some difficulty, Alma fought back the laughter that was determined to escape. She even managed not to smile, though the effort brought tears to her eyes – tears that Moira took to be of sympathy. When she managed to speak, Alma's voice was husky. 'What was Mr Fletcher's reaction? Did he see?'

'How could he not? He was three steps below me and my hands were full.' Moira's voice was tearful. 'He looked away and blew his nose, to gain time, I suppose. Then he took my arm and led me round into the little passage outside the toilet and asked me if I'd like to have dinner and go to the theatre with him.'

Alma had to clench her buttocks to prevent her laughter from finding another avenue of escape. 'You knew that he's splitting from Julie? What did you say?'

In Moira, shock had induced an attack of hiccups. 'Well, he probably only said it to make me feel better, though he did say that he'd always thought me very attractive. And I wasn't going to – hic – say that I wouldn't, because I knew about Julie and I fancied Mr Fletcher before ever these boys came along and I'd been hoping that he'd say something like that but not in those circum – hic – stances. He's going to let me know when he can get tickets. But, Alma, what must he think of me? What will he expect? Alma, what do I – hic – dooo?' She finished on a wail.

'You mean, if he makes a pass at you?'

Moira nodded violently.

Alma, while still convulsed with secret laughter, gave serious consideration to her problem. She recalled that she had considered sacrificing a virgin in Paul's honour and it seemed that she was to be given the chance to do just that. 'You should be so lucky!' she said. 'It's been an open secret that you were his slave from about two minutes after you arrived here. And very soon it's going to be make-your-mind-up time.

'It's very important that you remember three things. One: whether you do or don't is entirely up to you. Never mind what arguments he produces, the decision is yours. It's the one advantage that we women have. Two: if you decide the answer's yes, don't say it on the first date and preferably not on the second. You must, must, *must* be friends before you become lovers. Until then, try not to go anywhere private with him unless you trust him. But don't say no as if it's always going to be no, in case he believes you. Three: again if it's yes, make sure that you're safe. Remember: safe sex!'

Moira again looked blank. The shock of discovering that her precious secret was public knowledge might give her sleepless nights but at least it had cured her hiccups. Alma paused and looked at her, assuming an expression of severity. 'Moira, who did you bribe to open that door?'

Moira gasped. 'Alma, that's an awful thing to say!'

As soon as she was out of Alma's room Moira halted and leaned back against the wall. A trace of a smile crossed her face. For once in her life, things seemed to be going her way. She was definitely not going to turn chicken this time. She had come to a parting of the ways. It was time to leave behind the timid little schoolgirl and become a woman of the world, using the strength and wiles of womanhood to snatch what she wanted from life. Her breathing quickened and her knees seemed less firm.

Behind the door, Alma too was smiling,

but hers was a smile of pure enjoyment. Life had been becoming rather dull since she had decided that she was past the age for having lovers rather than revealing her cellulite to a comparative stranger, but now she could look forward to observing with amusement the progress of this little comedy, for several weeks at least.

Twenty

The burglar had changed his mind again and decided to enter a guilty plea. The decision was the sensible one. No court in the land was going to overlook the sworn testimony of eleven witnesses, twenty-two fingerprints and an unusually clear picture on security TV. Courts, moreover, go harder on the culprit when their time has been wasted in futile argument.

The decision also freed Detective Inspector Mills to do a little more about the Merryhill case. Nevertheless, he seethed with frustration. The DVLA in Swansea had furnished an almost endless list of owners of Shoguns but had then admitted that it could not provide, with any assurance of accuracy, information as to which of these vehicles were left-hand drive. What he needed, the inspector decided, was somebody well acquainted with Mr Merryhill and conversant with motor cars.

He found Paul Fletcher in his office, still trembling in the aftermath of his encounter with Moira. Paul had for some time been aware of Moira as a pretty youngster and a good worker, but the sympathetic vibrations between them had been offset by her habitually unisex garb. Then she had had a revelation, or had been kissed by a passing frog or something, and she had changed magically into a very pretty girl, verging on beautiful. Signals had passed between them that each had been afraid of misinterpreting, but neither doubted that a whole new awareness had sprung up.

The momentary presentation to him, almost at his eye level, of her tender little focus of pleasure, whiskered by a touch of youthful fur and framed by the secret trappings of femininity, had triggered the certainty that those signals had been of sexual awareness. His invitation to the theatre had been a reflex action. It had been something to say, a means of changing a subject that scaled the highest peak of embarrassment without it even having been broached; but it was not an impulse that he regretted. He felt that it must have been on the tip of his tongue for months. By her flouting of convention Moira had signalled that she was available and by her acceptance of his invitation she had admitted her availability to him. It came to him that she was at least as attractive as Julie and a fifty-times-nicer person.

He had thereafter had to face the problem of returning to his office. A man in a state of excitement can walk on the level without his state becoming too obvious, but going up or down stairs poses a different set of problems. It was for a similar reason and not with any intention of discourtesy that Paul received the inspector without rising. He indicated a chair and waited, his mind quite elsewhere.

'I have a witness,' said the inspector, 'who saw a Mitsubishi Shogun on Gledd Road at about the time of Mr Merryhill's accident. He is quite sure that it had a left-hand drive. Can you tell me of anyone among Mr Merryhill's acquaintances who drives one of those?'

Paul pointed out of the window. The inspector turned his head. Ernest Hendry, the other proprietor, was reversing his left-hand-drive Shogun into the building across the yard.

Mills leaped up. 'Thank you,' he said. 'You've been very helpful.'

'Not at all,' said Paul. These were the first words that he had uttered. He had been only vaguely aware of the inspector's presence.

The picture of Moira's trappings kept returning to him. How extraordinarily feminine were such delicate items! How charmingly impractical! They drew his mind back to an occasion during his student days. A flatmate had been getting married. At the stag party, the groom had over-indulged. Paul and the other occupant of the flat had brought the comatose bridegroom back to his bed. There they had undressed him and, as an afterthought, had drawn on his body in biro just such a set of suspender belt and stocking tops with the addition of a bra. They had spent some time embellishing their artwork with a faithful imitation of Brussels lace. When the groom had awoken, seriously hung over, and spied their handiwork they had told him that it was the work of the local tattooist. The groom, without pausing to think that real tattooing on such a scale would have left him in considerable pain, more even than the hangover he was presently suffering, had exploded into a tantrum of horror the memory of which still made Paul smile. The groom, moreover, had slept late, leaving no time for a shower that would have removed every trace of their handiwork and had been noticeably distraught as he went through the ceremony and the subsequent reception.

After a few more moments spent relishing the recollection, Paul picked up the telephone directory and looked for the number of the local theatre.

The inspector hurried across the yard and caught Ernest Hendry depositing a heavy parcel on a bench in a workshop that smelled of hot metal and chemicals. Hendry jumped when he found the large figure on his heels, but he led the inspector into a small, dark office. A practised swipe of the hand brought on two double fluorescent fittings and the men blinked at each other.

The inspector looked around curiously. The room contained a desk laden with papers, but it also held tables and open cupboards heaped and filled with metal samples and artefacts in every stage of development. There were clay and wooden models and casts in moulding rubber. Under the harsh light, Hendry's red hair seemed to blaze.

After introducing himself, Mills went through the usual rigmarole with his tape recorder. 'I notice,' he said, 'that you have a left-hand-drive Shogun. Were you driving it on the morning when Aubrey Merryhill had his accident?'

'Yes.'

'Along Gledd Road?'

'Yes. I had some reproduction ironmongery to deliver to the small builder who's working on Thripp House.'

The inspector was not accustomed to receiving such an immediate admission. He had to pause for thought. 'You did not come forward,' he pointed out.

Ernest Hendry looked surprised. 'I didn't know that you wanted to see me,' he said. 'The thing is, I've been away on business for the last week or so, so I just didn't know how things had developed here. I had no idea you were looking for the driver of the car. I would have come in otherwise, of course.'

'How did you get on with Mr Merryhill?'

Hendry shrugged. If the inspector's motto was 'Never explain', so be it. Perhaps some day he would want it cast in bronze. 'No problems. We didn't live in each other's pockets but we didn't avoid each other. We were just good neighbours on nodding terms. Sometimes we would collaborate on things like bulk-buying fire extinguishers; otherwise our businesses ran on separate tracks. If we'd met in a pub we'd probably have bought each other a drink.' Hendry paused. 'Aubrey was all right when I saw him that morning.'

'Indeed?' Mills frowned. His tidy mental picture was being blown apart again. 'Where was that?'

'Just beyond the track to Gledd Farm. He'd pulled off on to the verge and parked.'

Mills hid a sigh of relief. Hendry had passed the MG after the driver had been struck.

'What was Merryhill doing?' he asked carefully.

'Sitting there. I was tempted to join him. I thought that he was just enjoying the beautiful morning. He never even looked round as I approached, so I decided that he didn't want to be disturbed.'

That seemed possible. Aubrey Merryhill had not had that or any other thought in his mind. 'Tell me what other vehicles you encountered,' the inspector said. 'Meeting or going your way.'

Hendry had overcome some initial nervousness. 'It wasn't exactly yesterday,' he said.

'I appreciate that, but it wasn't exactly last year either.'

'I'll do my best. At least it helps that I don't go that way very often. Let's see. I came up behind a Telecom van and overtook it on the only wide, straight bit of road. Then there was an oncoming lorry after the road had narrowed and we both had to slow and squeeze past. After the track and the bridge to Gledd Farm there was Aubrey Merryhill's MG parked, like I told you. I didn't see any other vehicles between there and when I came out at Briggs's Yard.'

Mills hid his disappointment and prepared to rise. 'Nobody else?'

'I thought you only wanted to know about vehicles.'

'There was somebody?'

'There was the cyclist.'

'Nobody else mentioned a cyclist,' said Mills. 'You're sure that it was that day?'

'Oh, definitely. The road's narrow just

there and I thought that he was taking his life in his hands, passing that lorry. I overtook him just after I passed Aubrey's car.'

'The lorry driver didn't mention a cyclist. He just said that there was somebody waiting on the bridge.' A large man with an exceptionally deep voice does not easily sound plaintive, but the detective inspector's voice definitely held a trace of self-pity. A policeman's life, he felt with some justification, would be a whole lot easier if the witnesses would only tell the same story and stick to it.

Hendry shrugged. 'The bridge is overhung with trees so you don't get a very good view. He could have looked as if he was waiting, but he must have been doing his waiting while sitting on a pushbike.'

'Tell me about his appearance.'

'Have a heart, Inspector. He was in deep shade but dappled by a little sunlight filtering through the trees. And there was nothing to give any idea of scale. I wouldn't go so far as to say that he was average everything, but he wasn't conspicuously tall or short or fat or thin. I don't think that he was a black man and I'm fairly sure that he wasn't wearing a fancy uniform, but that's as far as I can go.'

'But it was a man, not a woman?'

'I think a man,' Hendry said thoughtfully, 'but I'm not sure and I couldn't even tell you why I think so.'

From his car, DI Mills phoned the Telecom depot. Isaac Barnes, the driver of the Telecom van on the nearly fatal morning, was out and about, but he was contacted and told to phone the inspector. The call came in a minute later. Isaac was adamant: no cyclist.

Mills returned to base. From his own office he tried to reach Henry Green. The lorry driver was out, but not out of the country or even out of the area. He was delivering bricks to a building site. The DI caught up with his paperwork and fretted until Henry called later that afternoon.

Without preamble, Mills asked, 'Was there a cyclist?'

'No.' (Mills's spirits fell.) 'But now I remember...' (They rose again.) 'I said there was somebody on the bridge. He was almost hidden by some hanging leaves but' – Henry's voice rose triumphantly – 'he was sitting on a bike. Either that or he had a third leg. And there was something funny about the handlebars.'

'What was funny about the handlebars?'

'Buggered if I know. They looked fat.'

Jerry Mills hesitated. He did not want to lead the witness, but he was waiting for a magic word. 'As if...?' he prompted.

'As if he was carrying something laid across them,' Henry said.

The detective inspector hung up, smiling.

Twenty-One

Lynne Merryhill settled herself into the same old chair. It had been several days since she last sat in it, so although it had no pretension to comfort it had some of the comfortable familiarity of meeting an irritable old friend after an absence. She studied her husband. The dressings were quite different and what she could see of his face was discoloured by bruise blood.

'Well,' she said. 'So you've had your surgery. And I'm told that it went "as well as could be expected", whatever that means. Doctors are very cagey about telling you what it is that they can expect. They probably mean no more than that they could sew the patient up and go home for dinner. I suppose that in these days of litigation culture they have to be afraid of being sued if they raise false hopes. They got rid of some splinters of bone, one very small leftover blood clot and some badly damaged tissue, relieved some pressure – and they did it all without cutting any blood vessels and you've still got most of the grey matter. Now it's up to you to heal and mend and recover your memory. They can't tell me how much you may remember. What you can't remember for yourself I'll have to teach you over again and you'll just have to be a good pupil in a single-teacher school.

'If your memory's really gone beyond recall, then we have a problem. But then, problems are for solving. I could, of course, tell you that you had been a magnificent lover, but that wouldn't carry any guarantee that the lie would be fulfilled. Even worse, it might set you chasing after every woman for miles around, unable to live up to the expectations of either party.

'I can, of course, tell you everything appropriate that went before, assuming that you're still capable of filing it away. But what do I tell you? The bad as well as the good? Are you memorizing what I tell you now?' Her voice underwent a shift. Clearly she was now thinking aloud, speaking to herself rather than to him. 'Can you remember what went before? Our wedding, for instance? If you can, surely you'll still remember it when you wake up. Conversely, if you're not going to remember when you wake, then you can't be understanding or recording what I'm saying and all you're getting out of it is the soothing timbre of a familiar voice. I might as well be reciting "Gray's Elegy" or reading from the *Financial Times*.

'In case you need reminding, it's been a good sort of life for most of the time. You've been a good provider on the whole, but we've had our ups and downs. I don't know what attracted you to me. I've asked you once or twice but never got a credible answer, just a friendly insult or a piece of conventional flattery. I've looked at myself in the mirror. Of course, a woman can't judge another woman's looks or even her own; I've noticed that women whose looks other women admire are usually butch-looking hags just as men often admire girlish-looking men. Whether it's direct attraction or the absence of competition, I wouldn't know. I suppose I look all right when I've taken trouble, but nothing out of the ordinary. Perhaps through the eyes of the opposite sex... I wonder if a homosexual sees his or her own beauty in a more flattering light.

'I didn't know what my voice sounded like until that inspector played part of my statement back to me. When I seemed surprised, he told me that one doesn't hear oneself through the ears but through the bones of the face. My voice sounds better than I expected, which must add a little to the impression I make in conversation. Perhaps that's what attracted you. For my part – and I can be absolutely frank as long as there's only about a one per cent chance that you'll remember any of this – I would have married Vlad the Impaler if he'd only take me out of what my life had become.

'As I said, it turned out quite well, most of the time. Our honeymoon was a definite plus at first. I discovered that I really enjoyed sex and you were quite good at it. We needn't have spent so much money on the hotel; we were paying for the gardens and the pool but we were hardly ever out of our room. We could see them from our window, of course. Even our meals came up by room service. We were at it like rabbits for three or four days, until you ran out of steam. I did everything I could think of to help, but it was no good. Frankly, I didn't have enough experience to be very clever at it. Really, I do feel that everybody should have some experience before getting married, or go on a university course or something. But of course I'm speaking of our generation. Today's youngsters get the experience, but that does not make them expert. I still think that a university course in creative sex would get most marriages off to a flying start.

'You should have accepted that no man could go on for ever. A rest and some rich food would have set you off again – as it did in the end. But you took it to heart. You moped. Then you began to hint at what you thought might turn you on. I was young and rather new to the mating game and I had nobody else to advise me. I had to ask you outright to be more open and you spoke about the benefit of what you called "loving bondage". You were so persuasive. You said that a little bondage, especially man tying woman, was a certain turn-on. The woman was freed from any sensation of guilt. How can you feel sinful if you have no choice? And the man has the converse feeling that his partner must be innocent, not a bad girl after all. I think those were the points you made if one peeled away the rhetoric you'd dressed it up in. Thinking about it later, I think the real value to you was that you needed to put aside your fear of rejection.

'You made it all sound normal and attractive, so I agreed. In fact, just the other day I came across a quotation.' She laid her book face down and open on the bed and unfolded her newspaper bookmark. 'It was said or written by an actor. I suppose an actor has to make a study of the seamy side of behaviour. If you don't understand it, how can you act it? It says that a desire to "devour, punish, humiliate or surrender" is pretty well central to a fundamental part of human nature and that it plays a big part in sex. It goes on to say that if you want to discover what normality is, you must study weirdness.

'I had certainly heard that many couples kept a few pieces of cord in a bedside cupboard. And, indeed, when it came to the point, there was a certain thrill in being at the mercy of a man. Fear itself is a thrill. The adrenalin rush that adventurers get is mostly fear. Also, it did bring you to the point just once more. But then...then you rolled me up on to my knees and laid into me with a leather belt. I couldn't even protest, because you'd taped my mouth by then.'

Lynne paused. She lowered her voice, which had become hard. There was a tear on her cheek. She put her hand on his and spoke gently.

'I can understand your motivation. I only recognized your shyness and your inferiority complex later. A chance to dominate somebody else must have given you great reassurance. If you'd explained yourself, if you'd been gentle, I might have helped you, even shared the fun. But you didn't and you weren't. I still remember the pattern of the bedcover and how the bed gave a little squeak before every stroke of the belt. I can still trace the marks you made on me that one time. I never let it happen again. I never put myself in the position in which it could possibly happen. But whenever we made love after that, I knew that you were fantasizing about that one occasion, recreating it in your mind – enjoying my pain and humiliation. Well, that wasn't hurting me again. You were welcome to that much stimulus, as long as it was only in fantasy. What somebody else thinks has never bothered me much. I find that what some-body else thinks I'm thinking is usually mis-taken, so the opposite is probably true.

'I loved you before that episode and I suppose I love you still, but it's a love born of pity and I never trusted you again.' There was a pause. She let go of his hand, blew her nose and cleared her throat. She folded up her bookmark again. 'I'll tell the children at the Mill how you're progressing. I'll tell you about them another time. I think I'll read a little now.'

The book of her choice was a robust adventure story, but her voice was husky.

Twenty-Two

Detective Inspector Mills's frustration was mounting. He now had a fresh lead and he should have been progressing at a gallop. The existence of a cyclist waiting on the bridge, then seen pedalling away from the already damaged car and driver only to vanish very soon afterwards was surely of enormous significance. This might have justified a request for the support that had earlier been his, though in the present state of workload he rather doubted it. He could imagine: *Sir, one witness thinks he saw a person with a bicycle waiting on the bridge and another saw a cyclist. We don't have any sort of description, but probably male. Of course, either of them might be getting the day wrong.* No, thank you. Anyway, Mills had little or nothing for a team to get its teeth into that he could not do for himself.

A little more thought told the inspector

that the cyclist, if he existed, was almost certainly Mr Merryhill's assailant and would have hidden himself and his cycle on the bank below the road at the sound of a vehicle. The inspector continued to think in terms of 'he' and 'him'. Without being sexist, he still could not imagine a woman cyclist swooping out of the bridge and down the slope, swinging some sort of club in her right hand, to meet and strike Aubrey Merryhill.

Thereafter, the cyclist could have continued to Briggs's Yard or returned in the opposite direction, or could even have made his way across the bridge and through Gledd Farm. Gledd farmhouse had burned down years earlier. The land was now worked by the tenant of the adjoining farm, almost entirely in cereals and root crops, and so was little frequented even in the course of agriculture.

DI Mills contrived to report that some fresh evidence was available in the Merryhill case without admitting how slender that evidence was. He managed to borrow a small team for two days and they searched the banking above the stream more thoroughly and over a greater distance than before.

They found signs that might have been made by a person manhandling a bicycle off the road, but the miscreant had not been so helpful as to drop any personal property and the area was far too great to be searched for traces of DNA, even if he had known whose DNA to look for.

The inspector himself looked for surfaces that a man might have gripped to save himself from sliding down into the stream, but he could see nowhere smooth enough to hold a clear latent fingerprint. He studied the faint markings that his helpers were interpreting as traces left by the assailant, but the steepness of the bank, the softness of the soil and the effect of the weather had caused a crumbling of the surface so that similar markings were detectable in many places. Fine weather had returned after a period of rain and with the lingering moistness of the earth he was sure that he was leaving more traces than he was finding.

DI Mills allowed his small team to return whence it came. He was left with only one question worth asking, one that he was perfectly capable of asking for himself: who had both access to a bicycle and reason to wish ill to befall Aubrey Merryhill? It was unfortunate, he thought, that bicycles were not registered, like guns and vehicles. To set a team to find out and list every cycle owner within cycling distance would be unprofitable, because cycles can be borrowed, stolen or transported in the back of a pick-up or on the roof of a car. He could ask that all officers on patrol stop all cyclists – and ask them what? Names and addresses – that would be all. A roadside check of each one of a thousand cyclists would hardly offer a propitious occasion for checking alibis and connections to Aubrey Merryhill. The list obtained would be huge and would contain the names of all the locals least likely to have known Mr Merryhill.

He decided to consult the one person who had, without even bothering to say a word, indicated the identity of the Shogun driver.

He drove to the Mill in his own Ford Focus and found Paul Fletcher dictating letters to Moira. It had become quite usual for members of the firm to exchange jobs as experience brought to the fore individual talents and task requirements. A lingering tension between Paul and Julie and the growing relationship between him and Moira had suggested that the two girls exchange responsibilities. Julie had proved successful and happy as Sales Director. A perk of the job was that it provided introductions to a large number of men, some of them single and most of them concupiscent.

Moira had an expert touch with the word processor, though she was not yet as quick as Julie. Between Paul and her there remained a sharp but not unpleasant atmosphere. Unspoken messages of mutual recognition, appreciation and desire quivered in the air. They had not yet managed their evening out; they had been waiting for the play that was being produced that week and Paul had tickets for the Friday evening. They planned to go straight to dinner from the office that day.

Each was therefore acutely aware of the other's sexual presence, more so after the delay. Paul, well aware of Moira's shyness and inexperience, was determined to proceed gently and carefully. Moira's intentions, subject to the manner of Paul's approach, might have been judged from the fact that she was dressed exactly as she had been on the fateful day, with the exception that she was now wearing underwear; and in her bottom drawer at home lurked some very expensive underwear purchased specially for the occasion. It had been made from a silk fabric so thin and clinging that the observer, had there been anyone so lucky, could have clearly seen the appearance of any goose pimples.

Paul had been insistent that the desk at the entrance should be manned at all times. But he had then called for Moira, who was doing that duty in the absence of Minnie Halstead: Minnie, being part-time, left at three. Detective Inspector Mills, however, already knew his way around the building. He found the office door open but knocked on it anyway. Paul was finding dictation heavy going. (Moira allowed glimpses of her upper thighs almost as frequently as Julie had done, but through inexperience rather than intent. Paul, who considered himself a judge of such matters, had been sure that Julie's legs were quite the prettiest this side of Hollywood, but he now had cause to revise that opinion.) He called the inspector in and offered him a seat.

'I've decided to seek your help again,' Mills said. 'The matter is very confidential.'

'Shall I go?' Moira asked.

'Can you keep a confidence?'

'She certainly can,' said Paul. 'I trust her with all my little secrets.' There was one little secret he was hoping to trust her with that very Friday.

'Stay, then,' said Mills. 'What I'm looking for is mostly local knowledge and observation. Just, please, not a word outside this room. I'm harking back yet again to what happened to Mr Merryhill. I've made a little progress. Two witnesses are agreed that there was a cyclist on or near the road very close to the time and place at which Mr Merryhill was struck. The van driver who reported the incident saw no such person. If everybody's recollections are correct – which, I must admit, would in my experience be unusual – it would seem that the sequence of events was this: somebody waited on the bridge, partly screened by overhanging leaves, until he heard the distinctive note of the MG approaching. I say "he" because this strikes me as a male crime, though I suppose that in theory a woman could have done the deed. Across his handlebars he was holding some sort of a club, perhaps a baseball bat or just a section of a branch. When he heard the car coming he pedalled out and picked up speed on the downhill stretch.

'Mr Merryhill was travelling, as he usually did in fine weather, with the top down, the windscreen folded flat, and he was driving at some speed. When they met, the cyclist could adjust his course to pass close to the car and swing his club so as to strike the nearly fatal blow, which would land with the combined speeds of the car and the bicycle. The doctors assure me that the angle of the wound was absolutely compatible with that. Mr Merryhill was unconscious but his feet were off the pedals – otherwise the result might have been spectacular, resembling the accident that the attacker might have hoped for. The MG coasted to a halt on the verge facing the stream. One witness passed it there without realizing that anything was amiss. The next passer-by realized that the driver was hurt and then phoned us.

'The cyclist, we think, heard the approach of the next vehicle and lifted his bicycle over the low wall or the Armco barrier, whichever there was at that particular place. He waited until he had the place to himself again.

'What I would like you to tell me, or to find out for me, is the identity of anybody who has the use of a bicycle and had reason to want Mr Merryhill injured.'

'Not dead?' Paul asked.

'Dead or out of the way – we don't know. It may or may not be significant that there has been no further attempt on Mr Merryhill in hospital. Generally speaking, hospitals are so big and have so many faces wandering around in them that not everybody can know everybody else. It is the one environment in which a man with a borrowed umpire's white coat could walk around with a syringe of something lethal – even air, if the syringe was large enough. But I have had somebody who you could call my agent keeping a lookout and nobody suspicious has even looked in Mr Merryhill's direction.

'It may be being assumed that as long as Mr Merryhill is in a coma he is no longer either a threat or an object of hatred to anybody. If he recovers consciousness, and especially if he is ever released from hospital – forgive my bluntness – we shall have to be careful because, in addition to the point you just made, the assailant may not be sure that Mr Merryhill didn't both recognize and remember him. I'd be happier if we could put him or her away before Mr Merryhill's release from hospital.'

'Why are you still saying "or her"?' Moira asked. 'I thought you were thinking of this as a male crime.'

Mills hesitated, but only for a moment. 'I am. But nobody had a good look at the cyclist,' he said. 'And I keep remembering that Mr Merryhill was inclined to be free with his hands.'

Moira hesitated, looking up. The men waited. 'Only in a friendly sort of pat-on-the-bum way,' said Moira at last. 'Not one that you could get angry about. Most of the girls said that he was very shy with them. They thought that if they'd given him any encouragement he'd have been too terrified to do any more.'

This insight into the mind of the injured man, coming through the lips and in the voice of the innocent Moira, was rather more than the inspector had been looking for.

'We'll help if we can,' Paul said hastily while the inspector was still groping for words. 'I can picture the use of a bicycle in conjunction with a weapon. It would be fast and manoeuvrable enough for a blow to be struck, polo-fashion, and a cyclist can escape in any direction including across country, probably without being noticed.

'Off the top of my head, I can only think of one person who might have wanted Mr Merryhill out of the way. That's Mr Stokes. He lives in the village. He owns the building, but we have tenancy on what I understand is an unbreakable lease. He came to see me here and acted in a very threatening manner. I suspect that he had already had a go at Mr Merryhill. I gathered that he wants the building back so that he and some friend of his can go into business together.'

'Doing what?'

'I haven't any idea. He was very secretive about it. I've been careful since then. I make sure that the last person out locks up properly and I don't allow any flammable rubbish to be left out with the bins – and so on and so forth, all as advised by the FPO. Anyway, I've only seen Stokes in an Audi. I can't imagine him riding a bicycle.'

'I can.' Moira suddenly seemed to be sitting on thorns. 'If it's the same Mr Stokes, and I think it must be, he owns a lot of property here and in the town. I share a cottage on this side of the town with three girls who work there and he's our landlord.

We pay him by direct debit, but some of his older tenants don't have bank accounts and he comes round himself collecting his rents. Parking a car can be difficult and the distances are small, so he usually comes by pushbike.'

'Well, well,' Paul said. 'This reminds me of one of those detective stories in which the character that everyone hates turns out to be guilty. That's Mr Stokes. It couldn't happen to a nastier person.'

'It hasn't happened yet,' said the inspector. 'He seems to have a knack of coming up smelling of roses, at least in one other case. It's no secret, because a garbled version of the story appeared in the local paper. He was almost prosecuted as a child molester, but the witnesses seem to be melting away. And, in the case of Mr Merryhill, it may never happen – even if he should chance to be guilty, which is far from certain. There will certainly be a delay, during which I ask that you each maintain a total silence about what we've been saying and about what I'm about to add. You see, there's a big case coming up and I've been warned to stand by to become one of the team.' He smiled wryly. 'This, you may be surprised to hear, is my way of filling in my time while I'm standing by. I will certainly have a good look at your Mr Stokes. I may have time to interview two people and then it looks as though I'll have to put it aside labelled "Too difficult" unless one of those interviews rings a bell.'

'Who's the other one?' Moira asked curiously.

The inspector looked shocked. 'You can't possibly expect me to tell you that,' he said.

Twenty-Three

Lynne Merryhill planted her usual decorous kiss on her husband's forehead before settling into the bedside chair. 'At last,' she said, 'you're beginning to turn the corner.' She looked around with satisfaction. The room could almost have passed for a domestic bedroom, now that they were away from the glinting fitments in High Dependency. The watercolours on the walls were unadventurous but colourful. The low window sill allowed the patient a view over a few roofs to undulating countryside beyond. It was a cosy countryside of small fields, hedgerows and strips of deciduous trees, quite unlike the prairie-farming that seemed to be taking over elsewhere. The golden tints of autumn were creeping across the land.

'I'm consulting my lawyer – that helpful young man who conveyed the house for us.

I'm instructing him to approach the National Health Service about reimbursement for all we've spent on your treatment. After all, they refused treatment at first on the grounds that it was a hopeless case. Now that you're pulling through it's surely obvious that the case wasn't hopeless and therefore that they should have provided the treatment. And you could have died because they got it wrong. I think that that entitles us to compensation as well as costs. I've told him to push it for all it's worth. He thinks it's a hopeless case, but he's going to ask for legal aid and if that comes off we'll try for compensation.'

She kicked off her shoes and put her feet up on the bed. 'You've cost a pretty penny, I must say. Not your fault, of course. You didn't do it on purpose. However, the business is doing better than anyone ever expected. We went into the red to pay for your surgeon and his travelling – he must have come by chartered helicopter, judging from the cost – but Alma's now forecasting that we'll be back in the black by March at the latest. A lot of that is down to Paul, but it's amazing how they've all pulled together since they got rid of that Streen boy. His father's a bad hat and the boy seems to be no better. The only danger is that, as has been pointed out often enough, there is nothing like an object of common dislike for welding a lot of discordant people into a team. With Garry Streen no longer providing that binding influence, will they go on working harmoniously together? Time will tell.

'There's one interesting legal point. I hope you won't mind my pointing out that the firm is becoming much more profitable because Paul's had the running of it. It could be argued that whoever put you in hospital did us all a favour, even including yourself. Common sense would suggest that any sort of damages would be inappropriate if you end up better off than you were before your injury. But the law and common sense are never within shouting distance of each other. Mr Beggin – our solicitor, you remember him? – says that the law would regard that as a fortunate spin-off. Claiming the cost of your treatment back is a long shot, but if we became rich as an indirect result, the law wouldn't write the one off against the other.

'The other children – I can't help thinking

of them as children – have been marvellous. There were a lot of small pieces of ostrich leather left over, too small to be used in handbags or briefcases, so they started making little oddments and stocking fillers for the Christmas trade. Bookmarks, key folders and funny animals – that sort of thing. Some of them are very clever. One or two of the youngsters have started spending their weekends going round the gift shops and taking a small commission in sweets or, I'm sorry to say, cigarettes.

'That fat policeman, the one who looks like a gorilla, was waiting for me at Maggie's house last night when I got back from the hospital. He was with somebody from the Met. I suppose he had to carry the locals along with him if he was questioning a suspect on their turf.' Mrs Merryhill produced a quite musical laugh. 'That's what I am: a suspect – can you believe such stupidity? He wanted to know where I'd been on the day of your accident, what I'd been doing and who I'd seen. I told him the absolute truth – that I'd cleared up after breakfast and then did a little gardening while I waited for Mrs Trimble to come in and start cleaning. She arrived at just about the time of your accident.

'That didn't seem to satisfy him. Perhaps he thinks that I hired a killer – what I suppose is called a hit man. He wanted to know all about our...what he called our "marital relationship".' Lynne paused and glanced down at the microphone that was almost hidden behind a leg of the bedside locker. She smiled secretly. 'I don't suppose that his interest was *entirely* prurient. It was almost as if he'd been listening in on what I said to you the other day.

'Lies and evasions would only have stirred up more suspicions in his tiny mind, so I told it all with embellishments. He was scarlet with embarrassment before I'd finished, but I don't embarrass easily and the man from the Met thought it was all very funny. Then the fat, ugly one wanted to see my bicycle, which is at home. He asked for my written permission to search the house. Well, he looks a little less trustworthy than that burglar they caught in the Morrisons' house, so I said that I'd be there this morning. That's why I was late; I hope you got my message?'

She paused. The man said, 'Umhum,' in what she chose to regard as an affirmative manner.

'That's good. I doubt if my bicycle gave him any pleasure: a very old sit-up-and-beg lady's bike that I hadn't ridden since about a year before we were married. With you to drive me around and sometimes a car of my own, why would I? The tyres were absolutely flat and God alone knows where the pump got to. I let him look through the house, but he seemed more interested in the sheds. He wanted to know what garden tools we had, but I told him that I left all that to you and Mr Jeffreys.

'I left him to get on with looking around while I started to prepare a room for you to come home to. I thought the other front room across from ours would be suitable. At least you'll have an outlook until you're back on your legs again. And the nurse could have the smaller room at the top of the staircase. What do you think?'

'Goo',' Aubrey said carefully.

'Good? That's fine. I've picked out a wallpaper that I think you'll like – I'll show it to you before I go and you can give me an opinion. I've started enquiries about a nurse, by the way. I wouldn't be able to do it all. The one I've chosen seems very

225

efficient, but if you try any bum-groping with her she'll probably break your fingers.

'They've all sent you their best wishes. Oh, and this is from Xanthic.' She laid a rosette on the pillow. 'He won a retrieving test at the weekend.

'We'll have to talk about Xanthic – the sooner the better. I know you two were great companions, but he needs a lot of walking and God knows when you'll be fit to take him for long walks again. I never was much for hiking, let alone that I'll have my hands full when you're home.

'Xanthic seems to be happy with Paul. We should think about letting Paul keep him and getting a replacement that doesn't need the same exercise. I've heard that retired greyhounds are very affectionate and don't need a lot of long walks. They're sprinters, not marathon runners. They get retired very young if they're not winning and there are always a whole lot of them looking for good homes as an alternative to being put down.'

Aubrey Merryhill began a rapid utterance of his present form of speech. The speech therapist insisted that he had made what she considered to be a great improvement, but it was not yet intelligible enough for the uninitiated readily to follow. What he was saying, to the best of his ability, was that if any living creature was going to make a one-way visit to the vet it would be Mrs Merryhill, long before he would consider exchanging his beloved Xanthic for a spindle-shanked greyhound.

Happily, his wife could only make a guess at what he was saying. 'That's right, dear,' she said. 'Think about it and we'll discuss it later.'

Twenty-Four

The outing that Friday evening began slowly. Each was aware of something life-changing on the horizon and afraid of deflecting it by giving an impression of unseemly haste. Moira in particular, warned by Alma, did not want to seem cheap. They ate a good meal in an overpriced restaurant, but talk between the two was inhibited at first. They talked about the news of the day, but even there the viewpoints of a young girl and an older man hardly overlapped. Just as Paul was thinking that they really had nothing in common but sexual attraction, another couple paused at their table. The girl had been at school with Moira and Paul had a nodding acquaintance with the man. To make a little diversity of conversation, Paul suggested that they share the table.

The gambit was successful. The other pair were into a number of outdoor sports that were enthusiasms of Paul's but that he had been starved of during Julie's reign. Moira had never been allowed into such adventurous pastimes and she was fascinated. As it turned out, she was a strong swimmer and at the talk of scuba diving over a coral reef she lit up. The wine slipped down like silk. Moira asked intelligent questions about diving, snorkelling and, as the meal progressed, bungee jumping and even hang-gliding. Laughter became general and the humour broadened.

At the end of the meal the two girls rose together. As the men stood, Paul asked why women always went to the toilet in pairs. Moira put her lips close to his ear. 'It takes two to tinkle,' she whispered. The revelation that she had a slightly ribald sense of humour set the seal on Paul's satisfaction with his choice of companion.

It was only a short distance to the theatre. They walked arm in arm. Paul and Moira enjoyed the play, reacting identically to each nuance. When it was over, they made their way within the crowd towards the fresh air, and by now Paul had his arm around her waist. He was quite prepared to summon a taxi, but Moira, who had taken wine only sparingly, had a driving licence. Paul's car was insured for any driver, though only third party. He trod on imaginary brakes, but Moira, as a driver, erred if at all on the side of excessive caution.

Sharing a small house with three other girls, while she could have offered Paul a last cup of coffee, the lack of privacy was tacitly considered to rule that out of court. Julie, however, was already in the process of moving out of Paul's house and, in any case, was weekending with the buyer from a major Manchester store. Paul's suggestion that he made a perfectly good cup of coffee was shyly accepted. Xanthic, eager to be let out, hurried to meet them at the front door but transferred his interest to Moira and offered her an enormous paw to shake.

'He's beautiful,' she said with evident sincerity, taking her captivation of Paul to a new level. He abided by the common male belief that anyone who loved dogs was inherently good.

They walked hand in hand, with Xanthic, under a moon so bright that it was almost indecent and they talked about the play. Moira had a keen and analytical view of it that earned Paul's respect. They took coffee in front of the television, not watching while a video played. When Paul, to bridge the first gap in their now animated conversation, made his first move to plant a decorous kiss on Moira, her reaction amazed both of them. Each had been looking forward to that moment all evening, if not for days, and each was psychologically and physically tensed up and ready to go. Moira's lips, soft and warm, were where her cheek should have been. In retrospect Paul was sure that, rather than his hands having found their way to her body, her body had found its way on to his hands. Such was the eagerness of both parties that the time taken from the first brush of lips to a complete and almost naked coupling on his broad settee probably still stands as a record. Xanthic dozed on the hearthrug beside them, totally unimpressed by these human antics.

Coupled though they were, they postponed the moment of climax again and again while they murmured and fondled, until at last it could be put off no longer. By then, Moira was on top. They came in perfect unison and fell asleep still coupled.

Impetuous though the first joining may have

been, Paul was gentle. They had savoured each other's body. Moira had been led by her aunt to believe that sex, if it ever arrived, would be a disappointment but a necessary evil if a husband's affections were to be retained. Her contemporaries had given her the impression that sex was violent, almost an act of rape. She was relieved and delighted to discover a whole world of unimaginable pleasure, to be given as well as received. Paul for his part was delighted to find a young partner who followed his lead as if on the dance floor but then responded with passionate enthusiasm. Julie had had her own preferences and had been selfish in insisting on their being indulged to the exclusion of any of any fancies that Paul might have.

The loss of her virginity had proved to be no more than a momentary discomfort to Moira, so brief that there was no resistance to the act being resumed still more slowly on their awakening. The systematic search for last night's clothes that followed was a game with no rules and no loser. It was only after a nourishing breakfast and an exchange of endearments that anything resembling coherent conversation became possible.

'You're delicious,' Paul said: 'sweet and juicy, round and firm like a peach. You must be the most...enjoyable girl in the world.'

Moira, though similarly inspired, lacked Paul's facility with words. 'You're terrific,' she said.

'Last night was the climax of my life.'

That said it all, but Moira, being female, had to have the last word. 'Yes,' she said. It was a good enough word as words went.

They finished the washing-up in cosy togetherness. Paul found himself at last able to think of something else. His native intelligence began to surface above the rosy glow with which sentiment colours the mating act. 'It's Saturday. I think the business could run itself for the morning,' he said. 'I'll give Julian Kennington a ring and tell him that he's in charge. What I'd like to do...'

'Yes?' Moira said. 'Whatever you like.' She gave a little shiver of excitement mingled with apprehension. She rather thought that they had done it all. What else could there possibly be for him to want to do? Carry her off to the moon? Imprison her in a haunted castle? Roast her whole and eat her with apple sauce? She had heard of such things, but only in video animations and horror comics.

'I would like,' Paul said slowly, 'to take a look at where Mr Merryhill was injured. Inspector Mills hasn't been given any proper support. He hasn't even been allowed to concentrate on this one case. I'd like to take a look and see if we can't work out the attacker's movements.'

Moira had thought at first that she was being dumped, but she took heart from the word 'we'. Her expression, which had been heading in the dangerous direction of a pout, broke into a big grin. 'All right,' she said, 'let's go and try. Mr Merryhill's a good boss and he's been very good to all of us. Not as good as you,' she added hastily, 'but good. Somebody hit him and tried to kill him. I think we owe him that much.'

'I'll run you home first. I love you like that,' he said as her face fell, 'but you can't go traipsing around in the countryside dressed like a...dressed like a...'

'Like a what?'

Whatever he said was going to be wrong. Even 'debutante' did not quite fit. 'Like I don't know what. You'll have to go back to your jeans and jumpers, just for the moment. I'll tell you when it's time for the glad rags again. Believe me, it won't be long.'

They were still holding hands as they walked out to the car with Xanthic neatly at heel – an accomplishment that Paul had taught him and of which the dog was very proud. He had his own rug on the back seat. 'The car's filthy,' Paul said. 'I'm sorry about that.'

'I'll wash it for you later.'

Car-washing was one task that Paul hated above all others. He would certainly take her up on her promise, but he only said, 'You should have a golden coach.' They kissed on letting go.

She left him to wait in the car for less than five minutes, which was quite acceptable and preferable to waiting under the eyes of three girls, all strangers. As it was, he was only too aware of their scrutiny from the windows. He could imagine the giggles. She emerged, sensibly dressed and pink of face, and threw herself into the car. Paul guessed that she had been subjected to an inquisition about him and their overnight activities. He hoped that she had given him a favourable mark. In retrospect he thought that he had probably earned it. He hauled his mind back to his driving.

They entered Gledd Road from the west, in the direction followed by the Telecom van and Ernest Hendry. 'Somewhere about here,' Paul said, 'Ernest overtook the Telecom driver. As I remember the road, this is the only wide and straight bit.'

Moira tried to think of something clever to say but failed.

They came to the mouth of the track to Gledd Farm. Paul turned in, crushing down a forest of dying weeds, and stopped. The bridge was so close in front of them that they were between the parapet walls and had some difficulty quitting the car without denting the doors.

'It must have been a tight fit for a tractor and trailer,' Paul said.

'There's another way in between the church and the pub,' Moira explained.

If there had ever been a cyclist waiting there the weeds had regrown. Paul supposed that it was too much to hope that the police had kept photographs of the area, but perhaps one of them might remember the condition of the weeds on the bridge. It was just the sort of place where an officer caught short during a search might retreat to empty a bladder distended by canteen tea.

Xanthic came with them on the regal principle of never missing an opportunity to take a pee.

A well-grown wild lilac tree leaned out of the bank and overhung the bridge. Paul moved among the branches. In the deep shadows the weeds gave way to moss. 'He would have waited here, probably sitting on his saddle, ready to go. There's a mark in the moss that could have been caused by a bicycle tyre, or almost anything else. If anybody noticed him, they wouldn't see him clearly enough to recognize him. He had some sort of club in his right hand or across the handlebars. When he heard the MG coming, he had plenty of time to start his run.'

'Mr Merryhill always drove fast,' Moira said. 'He took me to the dentist once when one of my teeth suddenly needed attention.'

Paul could see what she meant. 'The MG was quite noisy,' he said. 'I hope he kept his hands to himself.'

'He was the perfect gentleman. The road goes over a hump. The sound would be deflected.'

'I think that the sound might follow the valley.'

There came a mutter in the distance. It grew slowly then suddenly rose. A small motorcycle came into view, travelling only just, Paul guessed, within the speed limit.

'You're right,' Moira said. 'He had plenty of time.'

Paul smiled. 'Go on being devil's advocate.' He kissed her lightly. 'The tips of some of these twigs have been broken off. It's too much to hope that scraps of leaf are still stuck under his brake levers. Let's get back in the car.'

'You'll have to let go of me first.' The suggestion – and it was only a suggestion – was not invested with any urgency.

Paul was surprised to discover that his arm was round her waist and his hand was under her jumper. He freed her hastily. He would have to be more careful. He was not a new-comer to sex, but this was his first affair with somebody who clearly hungered for him and whose youth and love moved him as never before. It took an effort both physical and mental to move away from her. He thought that in a year or two they might be able to let go without a pang. As soon as they were back in the car they touched hands once for reassurance. The spark was still there. Xanthic, mildly jealous but tolerant, breathed in their ears.

Paul backed the car out into the road and let it pick up speed on the downhill stretch. They passed the area of bare ground where the MG had come to rest and then cruised on for fifty yards or so. Paul pulled up. 'My guess would be that this was about where the blow was struck. The car went on under its own momentum, but the cyclist must have been heading in this direction.' Paul drove on again until he found another place where the verge offered a possible halt and he pulled over. A knee-high wall protected the passer-by from the drop. 'Somewhere around here, give or take rather a lot, the cyclist would have pulled up. Or would he?'

'Well, he wouldn't want to go riding along with a club in his hands,' said Moira.

'He could toss it into the stream.'

'The police must have searched the stream. The water was low, so it wouldn't have floated far.'

'That's true,' Paul said. He decided that her shyness and her lowly job must have combined to hide a budding intelligence. 'And even if that's what he did, he wouldn't want to be seen cycling along this road.

He'd be in no doubt that a man would be found here, dead or badly hurt, and the probability that he had some motive for the attack would be bound to come out. By then he could probably hear the car and the Telecom van coming along. Somewhere around here the police found marks that might or might not have been made by somebody lifting a bicycle over. He'd get over the wall and wait until all was quiet again. Then what? Would he double back to where he'd started from, where we stopped earlier?'

'No,' said Moira.

Paul looked at her in surprise. She looked so succulent that he almost forgot to ask, 'Why not?'

'Just a moment. Let me think.' She thought. 'Yes. He'd want to stay out of sight. If another vehicle came along he'd go over the lip of the bank again, but between here and the bridge where we stopped before it's mostly that metal barrier thing that you can see under. He'd probably be safe enough, but he'd feel exposed. From here, this little wall goes as far as the footbridge.'

He was so lost in admiration for her reasoning that he almost missed the reference. 'Footbridge?' Paul nearly choked on the word. 'Nobody said anything about a footbridge.'

'I can't help that. The farmer put it up himself for the sake of his children when they crossed over to catch the school bus. It was quite unofficial – in fact it doesn't even appear on any of the maps. You can hardly see it now – it's all grown over; but it's still there.'

It seemed that she was not only bright. She was also omniscient. 'How do you know all this?'

'I grew up near here. This is where I used to play.'

'With the farmer's children?'

'Exactly. But only the middle ones. They had nine, mostly girls. The school bus stopped coming along here when they moved away.'

'Show me.'

They left the car where it was and walked in the direction of Briggs's Yard. Paul kept Xanthic strictly to heel. As Moira had said, the low wall continued. The ground was lower and fell steeply on the far side, offering concealment to a prone man. Soon they came to a dense thicket of beech hedge, which, Moira said, the farmer had planted to give shelter to his children while they waited for the school bus in winter.

There was a step behind the low wall and a narrow gap in the beech hedge, almost filled by growth. They squeezed through, scoured by the twigs, and cautiously descended a few yards of dirt path. The bridge had been built from rough timber, evidently felled for the purpose. It had been sturdy but was now showing its age. One or two timbers were loose and all were green with moss or algae. Beyond the stream, steps had been let into the bank and stone walls looked over the brink. 'That's where the house was,' Moira said. She put a foot on the bridge.

Paul was horrified. 'Come back,' he croaked.

'It's quite safe,' Moira called over her shoulder. Xanthic followed her on to the bridge, placing his big feet with great care. Paul dared not call him back. In his mind's eye the big dog would not be able to turn on the narrow bridge without putting a foot into one of the gaps between the boards.

Paul set off in pursuit, inch by inch. His head for heights, never of the best, seemed to have deserted him altogether. He might have crossed without fear if he had been able to avoid looking down, but most of the boards were slippery and some were either split or missing. The handrails on either side seemed too flimsy to be more than a snare and a delusion. He pretended that what lay immediately below the boards was a carpet patterned to portray a distant tumbling stream.

He tried to occupy his mind with beautiful thoughts. None would occur to him until he thought back to the few seconds spent disrobing Moira. That had, he thought, been reminiscent of unwrapping an unexpected present from fancy paper, rustling attractively and smelling of strange spices. He realized suddenly that he was nearing the far side, where the bridge had been engulfed, handrails and footway and all, by an ivy that had reared up from the embankment with the aid of some thin saplings. The ivy was slippery and it hid gaps in the boards, but it also hid the drop to the stream. Moments later he found that he had completed the crossing and begun to climb the steps. Some strands of ivy had been broken and the breaks were not recent, but he was not knowledgeable enough to judge the time scale. The police would have scientists available.

Twenty-Five

From the lower level of the footbridge, the walls of the farmhouse had given the impression of a complete and possibly occupied structure, but as Paul reached the level of the farmland he could see that the walls were all that remained. The roof, the floor and the windows had all been lost to the fire. Through the windows, where smoke had bloomed out to stain the old stone with soot, he could see bright-blue sky. The principal farm road ran from the bridge among the trees on their left and across the level farmland, between pastures and stubbles, towards the distant houses.

Moira had waited for him with Xanthic sitting beside her, leaning against her leg as though they were a long-matched couple. 'The farmer took some tractor parts into the kitchen to clean them,' Moira said. 'He had some petrol to do it with. One of the girls was making toast. The toast caught fire and lit the petrol. That was all it took. Farmers get careless about fire. Nobody was killed, but three of the girls spent weeks in hospital. I'd only just left to go home when it happened or I might have been burned too.'

That was interesting but only relevant in that it reminded him how lucky he was. He put his arm round her waist again. 'Imagine: you are the assailant,' Paul said. 'You have arrived here, complete with bicycle and weapon. What do you do?'

Xanthic answered only with a few sweeps of his tail, but Moira took the question seriously. 'I would have a good look around and if I saw anybody I'd hide in the remains of the house until the coast was clear. Then I'd get rid of them both and walk home.' She pointed towards where several roofs, peeping through a line of tree tops, betrayed a road. One or two windows were visible. At her gesture, two wood pigeons clattered out of the branches overhead. 'Then, if he met anybody, he need only say, "What a lovely day for a stroll in the country!" and even if that was remembered it needn't mean any-thing. Even a bicycle might start somebody thinking.'

'He wouldn't dump his bike,' said Paul. 'Buying a new bike might be seen as significant later. I think he'd come back later to collect it after dark.'

'I'm sure you're right. Let's go and look in the barn.'

'Barn?'

'There's a small barn beyond the house. We used to play there on wet days. It had straw in it and all sorts of fascinating machinery.'

With Xanthic in the lead they followed the remains of a path around the house and arrived at the small Dutch barn. A hen partridge retreated hurriedly in front of them with a brood of ten hatchlings, seeming impossibly small, scurrying behind. The hen dived into a patch of weeds with most of her brood close behind, but one chick was left on the path, panicking and cheeping. The hen led the whole brood back in a hurry while watching the humans with a cautious eye. The loose chick re-attached itself and they vanished into the weeds again.

'They've a good chance there,' Paul said. 'The cover's thick. I don't like to think of them feeding the crows.'

The barn was evidently still in use. The adjoining farmer, who now worked the land, took his machinery home, but the barn was used as a store of small and duplicate tools and minor materials.

Moira, with an effort, lifted a crowbar. 'How about this?'

Paul shook his head. 'Too heavy. And I suggest that you don't handle things. We don't want to get your fingerprints and DNA on the weapon if we do find it. Take a look at this.'

The floor of the barn was the sandy local soil. It held a fuzzy imprint.

'Cycle wheel?' Moira suggested. 'But it's not clear enough to identify the bicycle, is it?'

'I doubt it. But that might not matter. If this is what we think it is, the traces of this soil will probably still be in the tread of the tyres and between the tyre and the rim. Earth and dirt can be identified very precisely. This will be a unique mixture of the local soil and pollens plus any chemical fertilizers, weedkillers and insecticides this farmer uses.'

He had lost his audience. Moira was in the darkest corner of the barn. 'Look at this,' she said. Paul joined her and picked up a much-used pickaxe handle. 'Haven't you just done what you told me not to do?' Moira asked.

'Touché,' Paul said. 'But he would never have used this. It's filthy, and traces would have been left in the wound on Mr Merryhill's head. It's probably been in use here for fifty years. According to Inspector Mills, the wound was disappointingly clean. What... we...want...Aha!' He lifted a pickaxe by one of its arms. 'And I may as well tell you now that he wouldn't have used it with the head still in place, but if you give a pickaxe a bump on the end of the handle the head will come away quite easily and slide down. This handle looks new.' He carried it into the daylight. 'It's easy to imagine that I'm seeing traces of skin and hair, but I think we'll leave all that to the experts. There is one other thing.' He looked vaguely at Moira.

Moira said, 'What?'

'When the unpleasant Mr Stokes visited the office – not the last time, the time before that – it was Minnie and not you who brought him in. Right?'

'True. But I met him in the passage afterwards and showed him out.'

'Did you indeed? What did you notice about him?'

Moira frowned. 'Not very much. He looked much the same as usual, but I could see that he was in a fizzing temper. Is that what you wanted to know?'

'Not exactly.' Paul hesitated. He did not want to give her too much of a lead. 'His hands?' he said at last.

'I remember,' Moira said. 'He had a pink sticking plaster about here.' She touched the back of her right hand. 'I only remember because he opened the door with his right hand and the sun caught it.'

A smile spread over Paul's face. 'Thought so!' he said. 'I remembered that there was something about his hands. When you want to separate a pickaxe from its handle, you hold it by the metal head. If you hold the handle and bump it down on the end, the head comes sliding down the handle and can rap you on the knuckles or give you a nasty blood-blister by catching your skin between the head and the handle. He bought a new handle and used it. Then, rather than carry it away with him, he decided to leave it in the barn with other tools – the old principle of hiding a letter among other letters, remember? To confuse things further, he transferred the head from the old pickaxe handle to the new one.'

'Very clever,' Moira said, without explaining whether she referred to Paul or to Mr Stokes. 'But I don't think that the plaster on his hand was in quite the right place, the way you told it.'

'Then I probably told it too simply. There are dozens of ways to hold a pickaxe so as to give it a bump on the end of the handle.'

'That's probably it. What do we do now?'

'Just in case, we don't leave the clues unguarded.' Paul produced his cellphone. 'I call the police – Detective Inspector Mills, if I can reach him. We'll stand guard until they arrive. I think we may be able to amuse ourselves.' He took a seat on a tumbledown wall and pulled her down on to his lap. She was a willing captive. The sharp stones cut into him. It was agony and probably ruination to his second-best corduroys, but well worth it.

Twenty-Six

With a satisfactory end to the case beginning to loom, bringing in its wake an improvement to the statistics so despised by
Detective Inspector Mills, that officer had
been released, at least for the moment, from
the team investigating an attempted bullion
robbery that had led to the deaths of three
guards – an attempt that had links with the
funding of terrorism. He was warned to
wind his investigation up quickly. The
attempted murder of a minor businessman
was small beer in comparison.

This release, however, was immediate,
whereas laboratory reports might take some
time. If a fresh break were to occur in the
bullion–terrorism–murder case, such as a
lead to the dozen or more bigger fish who
had so far eluded the net as opposed to the
other dozen or so who had been scooped up
in it, his services would be required im-

mediately. Time, therefore, might well turn out to be of the essence. The DI sought and was granted warrants for the search of Mr Stokes's house and, if necessary and appropriate, his arrest.

There was no Mrs Stokes, nor even a mistress. The pretty young man who was his guest that week was subjected to investigation, but he had only returned a few days earlier from a long stay in Denmark. He was sent on his way. Mr Stokes was conveyed, protesting all the way, to Divisional HQ, where a room had been reserved for the interview. There, he was kept waiting until a search of his house was completed. His demands for the presence of his solicitor were unproductive. His visit to the police had been arranged for a time when his solicitor would have left the office and was known to be entertaining a young lady in a discreet club.

Mr Mills was ready to begin the interview. But first he stilled Mr Stokes's protests. 'Only the guilty need solicitors,' he said. 'Between us, I'm sure that we can clear this up quickly and you'll be able to sleep in your own bed tonight.' The implication that he would otherwise sleep in a cell was not lost on Mr Stokes.

Only then did DI Mills start the recorders and state the place, date and time and the identities of those present. He added the statutory warning. 'I expect that you know why you are here,' he said.

Mr Stokes glanced around the interview room. Its worn state and atmosphere of despair did not reassure him. He denied any such knowledge as the inspector suggested. 'I thought that that matter had been cleared up,' he said.

'What made you believe any such thing?'

Mr Stokes's voice became higher in pitch until it could well have been called a squeak. 'The witnesses withdrew their allegations. The whole thing was a put-up job intended to discredit me.'

DI Mills blinked at him. It seemed incredible that near-death had been inflicted on one respectable businessman just to discredit another. He decided to go very carefully. 'The witnesses were abiding by their signed statements up to yesterday morning,' he said.

'But Paul Fletcher assured me...' Stokes broke off. He could see broken water ahead.

Detective Inspector Mills sat up suddenly.

He looked quickly at the audio recorders and the video recorder. All were functioning correctly. 'What did Paul Fletcher assure you?' he asked.

Stokes shook his head.

Mills's voice descended into an even deeper rumble. 'Let me assure you that interfering with witnesses is a very serious matter, almost as serious as the charge you face of assaulting Aubrey Merryhill to his serious injury and danger to his life.'

Mr Stokes registered astonishment and indignation. 'Does he say that I assaulted him?'

'He has not yet recovered sufficiently to appear in court to give evidence. But he may soon be fit enough to be questioned.'

Mr Stokes appeared to relax. The inspector decided that this was owing to the possibility of a murder charge having passed by. 'Then there's no hurry,' Stokes said. 'You'll get the truth soon enough. I had no reason to hurt Aubrey. Not the least reason in the world,' he said. He decided not to try to claim that they were the best of friends. 'I thought you were talking about something else,' he said.

'What?'

'I said...'

DI Mills managed not to grind his teeth. 'I know what you said. You said that you thought I was talking about something else. I'm asking you what else you thought I was talking...' He paused. There was something missing. Ah yes. '...about,' he added.

Stokes again shook his head.

'Then you force me to assume that you were alluding to the attack on Mr Merryhill and that Mr Fletcher was bribing or intimidating witnesses on your behalf.'

Stokes's voice went up the scale again. 'No,' he wailed. 'It wasn't that at all. You are jumping to entirely unjustified conclusions. There was a little matter...quite different... You ask Fletcher. He'll confirm it.'

'Will he?'

Stokes hesitated. It occurred to him that Paul Fletcher might well prefer to see him on a more serious charge than that of feeling a girl's bottom. And it would be of little use to plead that his sexual orientation rendered him quite indifferent to the private parts of girls. He had been maintaining secrecy on that subject for years. 'It had to be a put-up job,' Stokes said sullenly, 'because everybody who spoke up at the time seemed to have faded away.'

DI Mills recognized the chance to apply a little leverage. 'I think you'd better tell me about it,' he said.

'But it was just a way to put pressure on me. Fletcher has some young women – young girls – working for him and I was trying to get vacant possession of the Mill.'

'So he did what?'

'Judge for yourself. I was in the town on business. I had just come out of the bank and was waiting at the kerb when a girl backed into me and then set up a squawk that I had – as they say – groped her. Which I hadn't, of course.'

Bearing in mind Mr Stokes's sexual preference, the inspector echoed, 'Of course.'

'People began to crowd around,' Stokes said indignantly. 'The girl disappeared and only the usual busybodies were left, not having seen anything but quite prepared to accuse me all the same. The case was allowed to drop for lack of evidence, but if real witnesses appeared...'

All was clear to the inspector. Paul Fletcher had worked his way out of a legal wrangle by framing Mr Stokes. All very naughty and possibly criminal, but evidence was singularly lacking. The inspector, who rather liked Paul Fletcher and very much disliked Mr Stokes, had no business allowing either sentiment to affect his actions, but policemen are human too. 'Coming back to the murderous assault on Aubrey Merryhill...' he began.

'I had no reason to dislike Aubrey. I told you that.'

'You prefer that we dispose of the question of motive first? Very well. You paid a visit to Mr Fletcher in his office and in the presence of Mr Kennington, urging them to give up the tenancy of the premises at the Mill and to allow the lease to lapse. You have just virtually admitted as much.'

'I did try to terminate their lease – that much I admit,' said Stokes. While he spoke, he was frantically trying to rearrange the true facts to show himself in a better light. A coloured gentleman who was notorious for running sweatshops staffed by illegal immigrants had offered a substantially increased rental for just such a building, well out of the public eye. 'A friend of mine had an idea for a new product. At the time, we were planning to go into business together. Just after my visit to Paul Fletcher we found that somebody else was going to be ahead of us with something very similar, so the idea was dropped.'

'What was this product to have been?'

Mr Stokes hesitated. 'I'm still bound by a promise of confidentiality,' he said at last.

'Even though the idea has been dropped?'

'It could be revived if our competitors hit any snags.'

'I see. And who was this partner of yours?'

'I'm not at liberty to say.'

DI Mills had been doing his homework. 'You would be well advised to forget your promise or to persuade your partner to come forward. Otherwise, you see, our suspicions are bound to focus on the fact that a major supermarket chain is busily looking for a site for its new depot. There is an excellent site between a major road, a motorway and a railway line, convenient to an airport and not too far from docks, but the Mill would have to be part of it. That project is still alive, but it seems to have settled on a part of Gledd Farm. You could have made a very substantial profit if you had been able to sell the site with vacant possession.'

Mr Stokes was short of breath. He could

feel a tight band around his chest and another around his brow. He had known nothing of this and suddenly the interest of the other party made more sense. He struggled to show no emotion, a self-destructive effort. 'You suspect that I attacked Aubrey Merryhill in the hope of selling the Mill?'

'The suggestion has been made. Shall we move on? Please tell us how you spent the morning of the seventh of April. That, in case you need to be reminded, was the day on which Mr Merryhill was assaulted.'

'Really, Inspector, I can't answer such a question from memory. If this discussion were being conducted in my office, as I first suggested, I could have answered you. I probably followed my usual practice of going into the office, which is part of my home, and checking the mail. After that, I would have known which of my properties I needed to visit.'

'By bicycle?'

To add to his other discomforts, Mr Stokes was finding himself in desperate need of a fart but was scared to release it in case it should be seen as evidence of the nervous stress that he was trying so hard to hide. It might even go into the record and be read out in court. He could imagine the reaction: *At this point the accused passed wind loudly.* 'I beg your pardon,' he said.

'You would have visited your properties by bicycle?'

'I often do. Parking can be difficult in the villages and almost impossible in town.'

'When you leave home on your bicycle, do you ever ride on to farmland?'

Mr Stokes was sweating although the room was cool. 'Never. I have nothing more to say until my solicitor is present.'

'It is suggested that you rode across Gledd Farm to the stone bridge and waited there. You were carrying a pickaxe handle that you had purchased three days earlier.'

'I have never made such a purchase.'

'We will see whether the shop assistant in Greenwood identifies one of your friends or contacts. When you heard the distinctive sound of Mr Merryhill's MG approaching, you rode out and picked up speed on the downhill section of road. As you passed, you struck him with the pickaxe handle. You could hear another vehicle approaching, so you lifted your bicycle over the low wall and concealed yourself until the road was clear again. You returned to Gledd Farm by way of the old timber footbridge and, in an attempt to cover your tracks, you exchanged the clean new pickaxe handle with the much older handle of a pickaxe in the barn.'

Mr Stokes repeated his demand for his solicitor.

'That is your privilege,' said Detector Inspector Mills. 'When you see him, you may inform him that skin and hair have been found on the heavier end of the pickaxe handle. They have been sent away for analysis and we are confident that they will turn out to have belonged to Mr Merryhill. Traces of blood and skin from near the middle of the handle have also been sent away for DNA processing. I trust that your wound is healing?'

Mr Stokes glanced involuntarily at his hand. The scar still showed pink. He closed his fist. 'I caught my hand on a railing while dismounting from my bicycle,' he said.

'We'll have the doctor take a look at it,' the inspector said. 'I may as well tell you in addition that a bicycle-tyre print was found in the barn. It was not clear enough for the bicycle to be identified from the tread pattern. On the other hand, traces of soil were recovered from the tread and wheel rims when you left it outside the bank earlier today. The laboratory technicians are prepared to swear that the mixture of sand, soil, seeds and agricultural chemicals corresponds with the floor of the barn. The farm tracks at Gledd are very hard, so that the sample recovered from your bicycle only contains a small addition of stone dust.

'Finally, I should mention that Mr Merryhill's memory is showing signs of making a return.'

Mr Stokes had appeared to shrink, so that his suit now appeared to be too large for him. The inspector's voice was hardening. 'You were shown a search warrant. A search of your house is proceeding. The men are looking in particular for the clothes that you wore that day. Yes, I dare say that they have been to the cleaners since then. But your bicycle has not and there are traces of sticky pollen and greenfly material left from your wait under the lilac tree. You were wearing a hat with a broad brim and we have hopes of finding the same contamination on that.

'You will be housed in a cell overnight and in the morning we will allow you to phone your solicitor. In view of the evidence piling up against you – and we have hardly started to look for witnesses to your presence on the farmland – your solicitor, when he arrives, might well consider the advantage of a guilty plea to a lesser charge rather than risk your being found guilty of attempted murder.'

Stokes sat very still. From the rigidity of his neck it could be seen that his mind was working furiously. At last he said, 'I wish to make a short statement. First, if you are executing a search warrant you are in a position to bring me my desk diary. If you do so, I shall be able to answer your question about my whereabouts on a certain morning. Secondly, my bicycle is not kept under lock and key. When I'm not using it, it spends its time in an open lean-to at the gable of my house. This backs on to Gledd Farm. Anybody could borrow it secretly.'

'Very well,' said Detective Inspector Mills. 'Your diary will be brought to you. You will also be given a copy of your statement to sign. My advice would be not to sign anything until you have seen your solicitor, because, frankly, the direction in which you seem to be heading would not convince a babe in arms.'

'Perhaps not,' said Mr Stokes defiantly.

'But an intelligent adult may be a different matter. It happens to be the truth.' He closed his mind to one or two minor exceptions.

Twenty-Seven

Detective Inspector Mills found Paul alone in his office. Paul was glad to be interrupted. He was finding, as many had found before him, that it was only too easy to promote yourself out of what you did well and enjoyed. As the managing director of a thriving and still growing business he could no longer spend his days making sweeping decisions or, as Julie put it, handing down tablets of stone. He had, he felt, become the repository of the contents of every staff member's 'Too difficult' basket. Even the buoyant mood resulting from the acquisition of a brand new friend, mistress, fiancée and slave sometimes faltered.

He looked up from a singularly badly-worded government leaflet about PAYE. Attached to it was a note from Alma Jenkinson to say that she could make neither head nor tail of it. The problem, he decided, was that it was easier to delegate upwards than downwards. He had nobody to whom to pass the buck – whatever the buck was in that context. Probably a dollar. Perhaps he should have Dave make him a leather chair back stating: *The buck stops here*, after the manner of certain American presidents. No, not a chair back – a seat. Much more appropriate.

For once Paul smiled on Jerry Mills's bulky form. 'Have a seat, Inspector, and tell me your troubles.'

As with Paul, when DI Mills was hard pressed he took refuge in humour. 'All of them?'

'You may as well – everybody else feels free.' Paul broke off, realizing that if things ran to form the inspector would take him literally. 'I don't suppose I'd have time for all of them. Tell me the ones that relate to us here or to Aubrey Merryhill.'

The inspector sighed, leaving little doubt that his heart was breaking. 'Where is that lovely young lady who was so helpful last time around?'

Paul raised his eyebrows. The other's words might have suggested that Moira's help and her beauty were truly appreciated, but his tone of voice suggested otherwise. Without comment he picked up the internal phone that had been one of his most recent innovations. He pressed a key, waited and said, 'Ask Moira to come down, please.' In the old days he would have stepped into the hall and shouted, which had been quicker but less suited to his new image. It was amazing, he had discovered, how the new technology slowed things down.

Moira arrived almost immediately. The smile that she always wore when joining Paul took a step back when she saw the inspector, but she sat down in the indicated seat and waited.

'Detective Inspector Mills is looking for shoulders to cry on,' Paul said.

'I would not have put it quite like that,' Mills said, 'but it comes very close. You, young lady, suggested the name of a certain gentleman as having had something to gain from the injury or death of Mr Merryhill and as also being the habitual rider of a bicycle.'

Paul felt it necessary to grab some of the blame. 'We accept what you say, Inspector, with one serious exception. You referred to Mr Stokes – you *were* referring to Mr

Stokes, I take it?'

'I was.'

'You referred to him as a gentleman. We do not recognize the description.'

DI Mills felt some slight lightening of the burden on his shoulders. He even managed a sort of smile. 'Off the record, now that you mention it, no more do I. But the fact remains that you put me in a very difficult position.'

'I apologize,' Moira said. 'Now, if that's all...' She made as if to get up. Moira's confidence had been increasing by leaps and bounds under the patronage of Paul. The old Moira would never have been guilty of such impertinence.

The inspector turned to Paul. 'Can you please get her to sit down and take this seriously,' he said.

'I might,' said Paul, 'if you'll only tell us what position she got you into, how she got you into it and what you expect us to do about it.' He made a downward gesture with one finger. Moira sat.

DI Mills's brow beetled. He knew that his leg was being pulled. These two irresponsible nitwits were high on something. He could have blown his considerable top. But he was in search of help; additionally, there was something about their euphoria that rubbed off on him. He had been young himself at least once and he rather thought that what they were high on was love. He spoke quite mildly. 'The position that she got me into is that she led me to believe that Mr Stokes was the guilty party.'

That made them sit up.

Moira's face fell. 'And he isn't?' she said.

'He has an alibi.'

'I thought that alibis always made the police suspicious.'

The inspector humphed loudly. 'They do. But this one could hardly be improved on if he had died and been in conversation with God at the time of the attack. He left early in his car, filled up thirty miles away at a filling station, where the cashier recognized him from his photograph. He even kept the receipt for the tax inspector. He then spent the rest of the morning negotiating over a vacant shop with the property manager of one of the big supermarket chains.'

'Well, I never told you that he was guilty,' Moira said in a choked voice. 'You asked which cyclist had anything to gain from an accident to Mr Merryhill and I told you truthfully...'

Simultaneously the two men recognized that the always emotional Moira was on the edge of tears. Paul grabbed for her hand while the DI hastened to say that he didn't blame her for a moment. Not a moment! What she had told him had been true as far as it went. 'But you can see my position,' he went on. 'I held him in custody overnight, had his house searched and made enquiries about his movements. That kind of thing can hardly be kept secret. There was even a paragraph about it in the local rag this morning. Unfortunately he has friends in high places. Just what relationship – but never mind that!' The inspector broke off hastily. 'Now he's threatening to sue. That probably won't come to anything, but he's making a complaint through channels.'

'We are very sorry,' Paul said. 'Two hearts that bleed as one. But I still don't see why you came running to us. We gave you honest answers to honest questions and it seems that sheer bad luck has led you up Shit Creek without the proverbial paddle. If you'll excuse me,' he added to Moira.

Moira said that he was excused.

The inspector was beginning to cheer up.

These two always seemed to have a cheering effect on him. 'I came running to you', he said, 'because my name is going to be mud unless I can find the real culprit. If I can do that, Mr Stokes's name will be publicly exonerated and as far as my superiors are concerned...'

'You'll shine in the dark?' Paul suggested.

The inspector even managed a faint smile at the imagery. 'I wouldn't say that – not by a mile. But a faint glow might be visible on the darker nights. So I come to you for your combined knowledge, both local and personal. Who else had motive and a bicycle?'

The silence became drawn-out. Paul was running his mind over various business contacts of the firm. Moira was considering people. Detective Inspector Mills's expectant look was fading. 'It was a long shot,' he said at last. 'But it was worth a try...'

At the same moment, Moira said, 'He doesn't exactly own a bicycle...'

'What?'

'Who doesn't?' Paul said.

'But he lives almost next door to Mr Stokes and if Mr Stokes was away, as you say he was, he could have borrowed his bicycle. You wouldn't know this,' she said kindly to Paul, 'being insulated from the manual workers, but Mr Merryhill was hard on him, harder than on anybody else.'

'Who?' the two men said together, producing a sound like a two-tone motor horn.

Moira came down to earth. 'Garry Streen,' she said. 'Alma says that he interviewed well, but that must have been when he was on something better than his best behaviour. How Mr Merryhill put up with him at all I just don't know. He's lazy and a liar and I don't know what. And he smells. I think Mr Merryhill hoped at first that he could make something of Garry, or make Garry want to make something of himself. But when that failed he didn't want to admit that he'd made a mistake. And I think he rather hoped that Garry would give up and go rather than wait to be fired and go to a tribunal or whatever they do. So he kept giving Garry all the rotten jobs and laughing at him and offering him up for derision by the others. Garry made pretence of not caring, but when he thought he was alone I've seen him cry. Really weep, I mean, with real tears. Anyone else, I'd have gone to see if a hug would help, but not Garry.'

'And yet he never did try to do better.'

Moira looked at the two men wide-eyed. Obviously such behaviour was quite beyond her comprehension. 'If he'd only done a proper day's work it would have stopped. But not him! I expect he thought that it would make him look weak. People are capable of very muddled thinking, aren't they?' she finished brightly.

'But you told me you saw all staff that morning,' said the DI to Paul. 'You practically gave each and every one of them an alibi.'

Paul screwed up his face as he thought back. 'I did see him. But I saw him first thing. He worked behind a screen, for no particular reason except that sometimes the goods coming in are packed in straw and we don't want that dust adding to the dust that's around the place anyway. Conversely, you wouldn't believe the dust that a very old building can produce and we do try to send out our goods clean.

'I put my head round the screen, wished him good morning and made sure that he had everything he needed and knew what he had to do, because the last thing I wanted was to give him an excuse not to do a morning's work. Nobody need have seen him if he sneaked out from behind his screen and he'd have had plenty of time to ride to Gledd Farm and lie in wait. He could have been back within half an hour. Even if somebody else looked round the screen and saw that he wasn't there, they'd only have thought that he was having a read and a smoke in the bog. And I'll tell you something else: he and Stokes were the only two people that Xanthic ever growled at. Xanthic, from the MG's passenger seat, must have glimpsed him arriving on his bike and taking a swipe at Mr Merryhill.'

'And Mr Stokes?' Moira asked. 'Xanthic growled at him too.'

'I suppose that Xanthic just plain hated him. It's easily done,' Paul said. 'I do it myself all the time.'

'There's another thing,' said Moira. 'For a few days after it happened, Garry had a sticking plaster between the thumb and first finger of his right hand. When he took it off there was a big, black blister.'

Detective Inspector Mills got to his feet. 'Now,' he said, 'you are cooking with gas.'

Twenty-Eight

'Did you miss me?' Lynne Merryhill asked, planting her still quite shapely bottom on a basket armchair. She felt good. She had treated herself to a holiday in the sun as soon as it had been made clear that her husband was well on the road to recovery. Her tan was still evident. Less evident was the lingering euphoria from two weeks spent in the arms of a Greek fisherman. She had felt entitled to a little reward for her patience and it seemed unlikely that Aubrey would recover his libido soon if at all. Months or years spent nursing a husband back towards health would be more bearable with a lover in retrospect and perhaps even another in prospect. She had her eye on the downtrodden husband of a neighbour. She thought that he too was overdue for an occasional indulgence.

Aubrey was sitting up, wrapped in a warm

dressing gown, in a more generous arm-chair. Several books in bright jackets were on a table at his elbow. His head was still bandaged, though Lynne had been given to understand that the bandage could have been dispensed with except for the sensitivity of the patient to the fact that his hair was in no hurry to regrow.

They had a sunny common room to themselves, smelling of warmth and floor polish. Beyond the big windows the trees were a mixture of green conifers, bare branches and golden leaves. There was a pause while he considered her question and searched for words. Speech was the faculty that was returning most slowly. 'Not much,' he said at last.

Lynne refused to be insulted. 'That's good. The Mill staff – the ones who knew you – all promised to visit you while I was away. I hope they did so?'

Her husband made the hissing sound that served him for 'yes'.

'That's good. But I phoned Paul before I came in and he said that he didn't tell you much about what's happening in the business. I think he's a bit shy about making money by going against all your principles.

The business is certainly making money or I couldn't have afforded my holiday. To tell you the truth, my dear, if I'd waited to *really* afford it I'd have had to wait until the spring, but I thought I'd better go while the going was good. They say that if you go on as you're going, you may get home in a few more weeks. I've got the nurse lined up and the physio will come in regularly, but that doesn't mean that I'll be able to sit and twiddle my thumbs.

'To tell you the truth, the NHS has been very good for once. Of course, the fact that they'd given you up and that I shelled out the money for your surgery had a lot to do with it. I only had to hint at having a word with the media and suddenly they couldn't do enough.

'But I was going to tell you about the business. Things are going wild in the run-up to Christmas. The idea of exchanging a handbag for a matching briefcase between couples seemed to be catching on, so Paul and Dave came up with the idea of a his-and-hers package with a purse and a wallet thrown in. That's going down so well that they've taken on more staff and bought a second-hand machine. They're having to hunt for fresh sources of ostrich leather and Dave's experimenting to find ways of faking up soft leather to pass for ostrich skin. But there are still plenty of small offcuts that would have gone to waste, so in their odd moments the girls are turning out bookmarks with funny slogans on them. Oh, and watch straps. People are even coming back for replacement key folders.

'Paul and Dave are full of ideas. And all the staff keep joining in. We may be in need of larger premises soon, so that unpleasant Mr Stokes may have the Mill back on his hands. The county council has factory units available only a couple of miles away.

'The equally unpleasant Garry Streen has been convicted of attacking you.'

''Member tha',' said Mr Merryhill.

'You remember him coming at you? I thought that that was probably what you were least likely to remember. Anyway, they didn't need your testimony. Paul and Moira dug up enough evidence to get the police hunting again and they built such a strong case that he could only plead guilty to GBH as an alternative to being charged with attempted murder. He says he only wanted to hurt you, to teach you a lesson. Apparently, he overheard you talking about him one day and so learnt that you were planning on getting rid of him. He's also obsessed by the idea that he's had a rough lot in life: an unhappy childhood, bad education, dead-end jobs. It seems he's extremely jealous of people who are more successful and richer than himself, which can't be difficult, to be honest. He comes up for sentencing next month. His habit of shooting his mouth off makes it almost certain that he'll get a lengthy stretch and a recommendation for minimum time off for good behaviour even if he behaves himself, which I for one consider less than likely.

'Mentioning Paul and Moira reminds me: they have decided to get married. What could be lovelier? The staff is playing it cool, but they're all thrilled and competing to make a big deal out of it. In their spare time they're making a very special set of luggage for the honeymoon. Julie's nose is a tiny bit out of joint, but she's still going with the chief buyer of a department store in Bayswater and he's letting her have a complete set of household linen, wholesale, for a wedding present to them.

'If you go on making the same progress, I

should be getting you home in plenty of time for the wedding. Moira says that she'd like you to give her away even if you have to do it from a wheelchair. We're giving them a full set of crystal wine glasses. Moira sets great store by nice things, so they should be able to keep them unbroken. I still think that we should give them Xanthic as a wedding present, but if the idea upsets you too much we could give them another flat-coat from the same kennels and think again about Xanthic when we see how you get on.

'I've checked to make sure that all the therapists you need are available nearby, though the NHS can't provide a speech therapist and we'll have to engage one privately. Your room's all ready. I decided that you wouldn't want a girlie decor, so I've chosen pale mossy green with touches of blue and some contrasting curtains.

'And now I think it's time for another walk with the Zimmer frame. Your muscles have lost a lot of bulk while you were laid up. Let's see if we can go right round the garden this time.'

1	21	41	61	81	101	121	141	161	181
2	22	42	62	82	102	122	142	162	182
3	23	43	63	83	103	123	143	163	183
4	24	44	64	84	104	124	144	164	184
5	25	45	65	85	105	125	145	165	185
6	26	46	66	86	(106)	126	146	166	186
7	27	47	67	87	107	127	147	167	187
8	28	48	68	88	108	128	148	168	188
9	29	49	69	89	109	129	149	169	189
10	30	50	70	90	110	130	150	170	190
11	31	51	71	91	111	131	151	171	191
12	32	52	72	92	112	132	152	172	192
13	33	53	73	93	113	133	153	173	193
14	34	54	74	94	114	134	154	174	194
15	35	55	75	95	115	135	155	175	195
16	36	56	76	96	116	136	156	176	196
17	37	57	77	97	117	137	157	177	197
18	38	58	78	98	118	138	158	178	198
19	39	59	79	99	119	139	159	179	199
20	40	60	80	100	120	140	160	180	200

201	216	231	246	261	276	291	306	321	336
202	217	232	247	262	277	292	307	322	337
203	218	233	248	263	278	293	308	323	338
204	219	234	249	264	279	294	309	324	339
205	220	235	250	265	280	295	310	325	340
206	221	236	251	266	281	296	311	326	341
207	222	237	252	267	282	297	312	327	342
208	223	238	253	268	283	298	313	328	343
209	224	239	254	269	284	299	314	329	344
210	225	240	255	270	285	300	315	330	345
211	226	241	256	271	286	301	316	331	346
212	227	242	257	272	287	302	317	332	347
213	228	243	258	273	288	303	318	333	348
214	229	244	259	274	289	304	319	334	349
215	230	245	260	275	290	305	320	335	350

Hu

This i
latest
perioc

- Ph(
- Visi